MAX SMART
and the
GHASTLY
GHOST
AFFAIR

Assigned to trail KAOS's top U.S. assassins to a secret seminar, Max and wife 99 board a train and start searching for the KAOS killer contingent. They are checking out passengers when lunch is announced. One by one all the passengers file into the dining car . . . and disappear! Rather than ignore the "drop-out" situation, Max and 99 report the curious incident to the conductor, who conducts them, at gunpoint, to the engineer— KAOS's fast-acting, antiseptic assassin, Arbuthnot. The train speeds to Arbuthnot's devilish destination—a ghost town with a small but spirited population: one ectoplasmic prospector and his immortal mule. Max manages to win the western wraith to the side of good. But can Max and his supernatural sidekicks stop Arbuthnot? And will Max ever find his Coolidge-head penny phone in time to summon the Chief and Control's counter-attacking counter forces? As usual, Max's blundering booboos and mindless maneuvers menace friend instead of foe!

Which all adds up to a ghastly ghost affair that's really out-of-this-world entertainment.

You will find the same absorbing reading and high quality in other TEMPO BOOKS. Look for them wherever books are sold. If your dealer does not have the TEMPO BOOKS you want, you may order them by mail, enclosing the list price plus 10¢ a copy to cover mailing.

A complete list of titles is available free from TEMPO BOOKS, Grosset & Dunlap, Inc., 51 Madison Avenue, New York, New York 10010; some of the books you will enjoy are listed in the back of this book.

MAX SMART
and the
GHASTLY
GHOST
AFFAIR

MAX SMART and the GHASTLY GHOST AFFAIR

WILLIAM JOHNSTON

A TEMPO BOOKS *Original*

GROSSET & DUNLAP • NEW YORK

A NATIONAL GENERAL COMPANY

MAX SMART
and the
GHASTLY
GHOST
AFFAIR

1.

MAX SMART, AGENT 86 FOR CONTROL, trotted down the steps from the upper floor of his apartment, then halted at the landing and glanced out the window. He was pleased to see that the sun was out and the sky was clear. So far, so good, he thought. He had been up for nearly a half-hour, and, as yet, nothing startling or disastrous had occurred. Perhaps one of those days unlike any other day was beginning. Maybe this Monday would go down in the annals of—

As Max started down the short flight of stairs that led to the foyer and the living room, he heard a noise from the direction of the kitchen. Quickly, trained to act without thinking, he flattened himself against a wall and whipped out his pistol. He heard the noise again. It sounded like pans rattling. Slowly, pistol at the ready, Max moved toward the kitchen.

As he reached the kitchen doorway, he heard the sound once more. Max took in a deep breath, then threw the door open—and found himself face to face with the intruder in his kitchen. She was a strikingly attractive young woman, with dark hair and soft dark eyes, and a particularly fetching smile.

"Good-morning, Max," the young woman said, smiling fetchingly and pushing his pistol aside. "What would you like for breakfast?"

Max looked sheepish. "I'm sorry I keep doing that, 99," he said to his wife, putting the gun away. "It's just that it's very difficult for me, in some ways, to get used to being married. Before, when I heard sounds in the morning in the kitchen, it was always a KAOS agent waiting to assassinate me. So, when I went in to put on breakfast, I'd draw first and plug in the coffee-maker second. Old habits are difficult to break."

"Well, from now on, it will be me in the kitchen," 99 said. "See? There are a lot of advantages to being married. Now, Max, what would you like for breakfast?"

"Oh, the same," Max replied, "coffee and toast." He headed toward the living room. "I'll have it out here," he said.

"Max, coffee and toast aren't enough," 99 said, following him. "You need more nourishment. After all, you lead a strenuous life."

"All right," Max said. "Instead of coffee and toast, I'll have *potage bisque de homard, filet de boeuf à la façon des natues, puree de marrons* and *omelette Alaska.*"

99 stared at him wide-eyed. "Max—what's that?"

"Well, that's lobster bisque, fillet of beef, chestnut puree and baked Alaska."

"Max, I asked for a suggestion for breakfast, not for a banquet at the French consulate."

"You said I need more nourishment, 99. You can't say what I suggested wouldn't be nourishing."

"Would you settle for toast and coffee, Max?"

He nodded. "I'll have toast and coffee, 99."

"Right," 99 said, heading back toward the kitchen.

"Toast and coffee for three." She entered the kitchen and the door closed behind her.

Max frowned. Then, using his fingers, he added up the number of occupants in the apartment. It came to two. Yet, 99 had said 'toast and coffee for *three.*' Obviously, they were going to have a visitor.

Max returned to the kitchen doorway and stood in the opening. "That was very cute, 99, the way you told me that," he said. "I like the modern way best. In the old days, the wife used to let her husband discover the knitting. This is much better. Because the knitting might be around for years and I would never see it. I might discover the knitting *needles,* but the knitting itself, no. When are you due?"

99 had been dropping bread into the toaster but had stopped to turn to Max and look at him puzzledly. "Max, when am I due for what? What are you talking about?"

"I'm talking about the little visitor you're expecting," Max replied. "You just told me about it, in your cute little way, when you said 'toast and coffee for three.' "

"Max, the visitor I'm expecting isn't exactly little. It's the Chief. He called while you were in the shower and said for us to wait here for him."

"Oh," Max replied, mildly disappointed. "Well, it's probably just as well. If it was the other kind of visitor, I imagine he, she or it would be too young for toast and coffee." He thought a moment, then said, "This is one of the advantages of being married that I'm really going to like."

"What's that, Max?"

"Having the Chief come here instead of us going to the office," Max replied. "No more fighting that morning traffic. No more punching that time clock. This will be great!"

"Max, it's only *this* morning that he'll be coming

here. Normally, we'll go to the office just as usual. He said he has a new assignment for us, and we'll be able to leave from here just as well as from the office. I think it's—"

The doorbell chimed.

"That's probably the Chief, Max."

"No, I think it was the doorbell, 99. The doorbell chimes. The Chief just sort of groans. You can tell the difference by listening to— Oh, yes, I see what you mean—"

Max left the kitchen and went to the door and disengaged the several locks, then opened the door a crack and peeked out. The Chief of Control was there.

"Hi, Chief," Max said. "We don't have a password here, so we'll have to skip that part of our morning meeting."

"Good, Max—just open the door."

"How will I know if you're friend or foe if we don't have a password?" Max asked, keeping the door closed except for the crack. "You could be a KAOS agent disguised as the Chief, you know."

The Chief was frowning, sniffing the air. "Max, I think the toast is burning," he said.

Max opened the door. "That's the password," he said. Then, as the Chief entered, he called out to 99. "99, the password is burning!"

"I know!" 99 called back. "Don't worry—I'm adding a little more water!"

"I guess it wasn't the toast that was burning, it was the coffee," Max said to the Chief.

The Chief looked perplexed. "Max, it's toast that burns. I don't think coffee ever burns."

"Well, 99 is sort of new at this," Max explained. "She probably doesn't know that yet." He motioned to a chair. "Have a seat, Chief. Breakfast is coming right up. How would you like ham and eggs and fried potatoes and toast and marmalade?"

The Chief beamed. "That sounds wonderful, Max!"

"Okay, we'll go out to a restaurant," Max said. "Just a minute—I'll tell 99 we're leaving."

"No, Max! Don't—"

The kitchen door opened at that moment, and 99 came out. She was carrying a large tray. On it was a stack of toast and a coffee urn and cups and saucers and sugar and cream.

" 'Morning, Chief," 99 said, placing the tray on the low table in front of his chair. "I'm sorry I don't have a bigger breakfast to offer you. But I sort of wasn't expecting company."

"That's all right, 99—this looks fine," the Chief said. "The *potage bisque de homard, filet de boeuf à la façon des natues, puree de marrons* and *omelette Alaska* I usually have for breakfast always leave me with a stuffed feeling, anyway."

"What's the assignment, Chief?" Max asked, as 99 poured the coffee.

"Well, Max—"

"Have some coffee, Chief," 99 said.

"What? Oh . . . yes, all right." He lifted the cup and sipped. Then, putting it down, he started to continue the reply to Max. "This assignment—"

"How was it, Chief?" 99 broke in.

The Chief looked a little uncomfortable. "Frankly, 99, it tasted a little burned," he replied.

"I was afraid of that," 99 said, annoyed.

"What was it you were saying about the assignment, Chief?" Max said.

"Oh . . . yes . . . Well, this assignment—"

"Try the toast, Chief," 99 interrupted.

Resigned, the Chief picked up a slice of toast and tasted it. "I'm sorry, 99, but it's a little weak," he told her.

"I knew it!" she said. "I added too much water."

"99, would you please let the Chief tell us about the assignment?" Max said.

"I'm sorry," 99 said. "Go on, Chief."

"Well, Max . . . 99 . . . we've learned that sometime within the next few days every KAOS assassin in the U.S. will be gathered in one place. And—what may be even more important—KAOS' top international assassin, Arbuthnot, will be there, too. As you can easily see, it will be a golden opportunity for Control."

Max frowned. "I don't quite see it, Chief."

"Max—think. It's going to be kind of a seminar meeting. In other words, Arbuthnot, the top international assassin, will be lecturing to all the top U.S. assassins on the latest advancements in the assassination game. They'll all be together for several days, probably. Do you see now why I say it's a golden opportunity for Control?"

"You mean we're going to cater it, Chief?"

"No, Max! I mean it's a golden opportunity for us to eliminate not only all the top U.S. assassins, but also KAOS' top international assassin! Wouldn't you call that a golden opportunity?"

"You mean we're going to assassinate the assassins, Chief?" Max said.

"No . . . we won't do that. Not unless it's absolutely necessary. We'll just take them captive, then we'll re-educate them, so that, from then on, they'll be harmless."

"Brainwash them, you mean," 99 said.

The Chief shook his head. "No, 99, I mean re-educate them. When KAOS does it, it's brainwashing. When we do it, it's re-educating."

99 nodded. "I'll remember that," she said. "Where will all these assassins be, Chief?"

"Well . . . that, I don't know," the Chief replied. "All we know is that the top U.S. assassins have collected here in Washington and that they're going to take a train to New York this afternoon."

"That's the dumbest thing I ever heard of," Max said.

The Chief and 99 peered at him. "Max, what's so dumb about taking a train to New York?" the Chief asked.

"It's as dumb as carrying coals to Newcastle," Max replied. "There are plenty of trains in New York. Why not get one when they get there, instead of carrying one all the way from Washington. Besides, how will they ever get it on the plane? Isn't there a limit on the amount of baggage you can—" He suddenly brightened. "Oh! I see. You mean they're going to *ride* a train to New York. Why didn't you say so, Chief? You know, there's a big difference between—"

"Max!

"I'm sorry, Chief. But be a little more careful of your wording from now on, will you?"

"I'll put it this way:" the Chief said. "This afternoon, KAOS' top U.S. assassins will board a train in Washington that is scheduled to depart for New York. We don't know what their final destination will be. They might get on the train, and then immediately get off. Or, they might ride it to the first stop . . . or the second or third stop . . . They might go all the way to New York, then transfer to another train or to a plane or— My point is, the only thing we know for sure about their transportation plans is that they have tickets for that train this afternoon. Is that clear?"

"You certainly go into a lot of detail to say you don't know anything, Chief," Max commented. "Too much detail can be confusing, you know. When you have nothing to say, it's best to say it in the briefest possible way. A tidy mind is a sign of intelligence. I don't mean to infer by that that you're not intelligent though. What it probably is, I think, is a basic lack of

confidence in your associates' ability to comprehend.
This is indicated by your question as the end of the explanation. You went into all that detail, and you were
very explicit about it, and then you said, 'Is that clear?'
In other words, you were asking us if we understood
all the things you had told us. Now, that was hardly
necessary. You were so specific about everything, even
an idiot would have understood. Yet, you were unable
to accept the obvious: that is, the fact that you were
speaking to highly-trained, extraordinarily perceptive—"

"Max," the Chief broke in, "will you just answer the
question? Was it clear?"

"Was *what* clear, Chief?"

The Chief turned to 99. "You understood it, I'm
sure," he said. "Please explain it to Max after you get
aboard the train."

99 nodded. "Of course, Chief." She indicated his
empty cup. "Would you like some more coffee?"

"Yes . . . thank you . . ."

99 picked up the Chief's cup and saucer and then
started to pick up the coffee urn. But at that instant
the Chief's chair suddenly tipped backwards, flipping
him out and across the room. He crashed into a corner, then lay there, stunned.

Max and 99 got up quickly and ran to him.

"Chief! Are you all right?" Max asked.

The Chief opened his eyes. "Yes . . ." he replied
dimly. "I . . . what happened?"

"I'm sorry, Chief . . . it was my fault," 99 said. "I'm
still not used to this apartment. Every once in a while,
I activate one of Max's booby traps—unintentionally,
of course." She looked at Max. "What did I do that
time?" she asked.

"You broke the electric eye beam when you waved
that coffee cup around," Max explained. "It causes the
chair to flip over backwards, usually breaking somebody's leg."

"The leg of whoever's in the chair, you mean?"

"No, the leg of whoever gets hit by whoever's in the chair," Max replied. He turned his attention to the Chief once more. "How are your legs, Chief?" he asked.

"I think I survived without any damage," he replied, getting to his feet.

"That's a break," Max said. "Or, to put it another way, that's *not* a break."

Max and 99 helped the Chief back to the chair.

"Do you want that coffee now, Chief?" 99 asked when he was seated again.

"No, no," he said quickly. "Just let me finish telling you about this assignment so I can get out of here. Now, do you understand what it is you're supposed to do? I have tickets for you for that train. You'll go aboard and you'll try to locate the KAOS assassins. Then—"

"How will we identify them, Chief?" Max asked. "Will they have badges pinned to their lapels?"

"Max, why would they have badges pinned to their —Oh, you mean because they are going to a meeting." He shook his head. "No, Max, they won't have badges. I don't know how you'll identify them. I don't have pictures of them, I don't have descriptions. Nothing. All I know is that they'll be on that train."

"I see," Max nodded. "We'll have to depend on training and intelligence to spot them."

"Well . . . training, yes," the Chief replied. "Now—" He suddenly winced and put a hand on his back. "I think I must have sprained something when this chair threw me," he said.

"Here, Chief," 99 said, reaching for a pillow on the sofa. "Put this behind your—"

"No, 99!" Max shouted.

But the warning was too late. The chair flipped the Chief foward and he dived across the low table, sending cups and saucers and the coffee urn and toast and coffee and sugar and cream in all directions. He ended up in another corner, stunned.

Max and 99 raced to him.

"Chief—are you all right?" Max asked.

He opened his eyes. "Yes . . . I . . . what happened?"

"My fault again, Chief," 99 said apologetically. "I forgot what happens when that pillow is moved. Did you break anything this time?"

"I don't know—did I? It sounded like china shattering."

"Don't worry about that. I mean *you*," 99 said. "Try to stand up."

The Chief shook his head. "No. I'm going to stay right here in the corner until I finish filling you in on this assignment," he said. "If I don't, I'll be going to a hospital instead of back to headquarters when I leave here. Now . . . where was I?"

"You were diving across the coffee table, Chief," Max told him. "And very gracefully, too—considering, of course, that you weren't prepared for it."

"I mean where was I in the briefing?"

"Oh. Well, you'd just told us that the KAOS assassins won't be wearing badges."

"That's right," the Chief nodded. "I can't suggest any way to identify them. They'll probably look like common ordinary everyday people. But, somehow, you'll have to locate them on that train, and then follow them wherever they go. That's the important thing. We have to find out where that meeting is being held."

"Chief, there's an easier way, you know," Max said.

"There is—how?"

"Well, we know the assassins will be on the train," Max said. "So, why don't we just take *all* the passengers into custody and re-educate them all? That way, we'd be bound to get the assassins."

"Max . . . I'm afraid that would get us into a bit of trouble."

"How? Who would tell? All the passengers would be re-educated. They wouldn't know what happened to them."

"No, Max, we can't do that," the Chief said. "Besides, it wouldn't be a guarantee of success. You see, it's Arbuthnot we really want the most. He knows more about assassination than any man alive. If we could snare him and then relieve him of all that information— Well, obviously, it would be a great day for Control."

"That makes my idea all the better," Max said. "If we took all the passengers into custody, we'd get Arbuthnot, too. How could we miss?"

"Max, we're not sure that Arbuthnot will be on the train. The KAOS communication we intercepted ordered all the U.S. assassins to take that train, but there was no mention of Arbuthnot. He might be flying to the meeting place. Or hitchhiking, for all we know."

Max sighed. "Okay, I guess we'll have to do it the hard way," he said. "Now, let me get it straight. We board the train and then we come back here to the apartment. After—"

"Max, no!" the Chief broke in. "Why come back here to the apartment?"

"To get the tickets," Max replied. "I always forget the tickets."

"I'll take the tickets, Max," 99 said. "After all, what's a wife for?"

"Okay," Max said. "We board the train and we locate the KAOS assassins. We stay with them until they arrive at the meeting place, then we go to the nearest telephone—"

"No, Max," the Chief interrupted again.

"You're right, Chief. We locate them, then I call you on my shoe phone. Then—"

"No, Max," the Chief said.

"Do we locate them?" Max asked.

"Yes, that part is correct," the Chief nodded. "But it probably won't be possible for you to telephone me. KAOS has developed a communications neutralizer. It can make all the normal means of communication for miles around inoperative. They will undoubtedly have a communications neutralizer at the meeting place. So, you will not be able to phone me or telegraph me."

"I could write you a letter," Max suggested.

"These days, it would take too long to reach me."

"Smoke signals?"

"No, Max. But there is a way." The Chief got what looked like a coin from his pocket and handed it to Max. "What does this look like?" he said.

Max scrutinized it closely for a second. "A penny?"

"Yes . . . but what kind of a penny, Max?"

Max turned the coin over and over. "An Indian-head penny?" he guessed.

"Max, look closer."

"Oh, yes . . . I see . . ." Max said after a second. "That's not an Indian, is it? It's . . . now, don't tell me—I know him. I've seen him in old newsreels . . . wearing that Indian head-dress. It's . . . uh . . ." He shrugged. "I give up."

"Max, that's a Coolidge-head penny," the Chief said.

"Sure! That's right. How many of these did they mint, Chief?"

"None!" the Chief replied. "That's the only Coolidge-head penny in existence, Max. We made it that way so you could carry it in your pocket and yet identify it quickly when you needed it. Do you have any idea what it *really* is?"

Max inspected the penny again. "A Hoover-head nickel?" he guessed.

"No! It's a communications neutralizer neutralizer!"

"Oh . . . sure . . ." Max nodded. "I see. With this Coolidge-head penny, I can neutralize KAOS' communications neutralizer, and then the phones will work."

"Even better than that, Max," the Chief said. "When you rub that penny it sends out a signal. That signal will be picked up at Control headquarters. Then, we'll be able to home in on it and locate the meeting place and take all those KAOS assassins—including Arbuthnot—into custody."

"That's wonderful, Chief!" 99 said.

"That's more than Coolidge was able to do," Max said. He dropped the penny into his pocket. "Is there anything else, Chief?"

"No," the Chief replied. "Just . . . just help me up . . . and let me get out of here before any more of those booby traps go off."

Max and 99 assisted the Chief in getting to his feet, then walked to the door with him.

"The tickets are in here," the Chief said, handing 99 an envelope. "Don't miss that train."

"Don't worry, Chief."

Max opened the door. "Sure you wouldn't like to take a doggy bag of toast and coffee with you?" he said.

"Yes, I'm pretty sure about that," the Chief replied. He stepped out into the corridor. "Don't forget, now —we'll be waiting for that signal at headquarters."

"Got it," Max nodded. "So long, Chief," he said, starting to close the door.

"Oh . . . and drop in anytime, Chief!" 99 called.

"No, 99!" Max said.

From the corridor came the sound of a crash. Then the Chief could be heard expressing himself in a way that indicated a certain degree of dissatisfaction with current conditions.

"What happened?" 99 asked Max, baffled.

"That's a booby trap I forgot to tell you about,"

Max explained. "Never say 'Drop in anytime' to anyone who's leaving, 99. That particular phrase trips a
trap door in the corridor."

99 looked, horrified, at the closed door. The Chief's
complaints could still be heard—but much more
faintly now. "Max, we better do something!"

"That's been taken care of," Max informed her,
turning away. "The trap door opens into a doctor's office on the ground floor. By now, the Chief is in good
hands."

2.

MAX AND 99 SPENT THE REST of the morning packing. It took considerable time because they were not sure where they were going. As the Chief had pointed out, the train might take the KAOS assassins only on the first leg of the trip to the meeting site. Consequently, Max and 99 might end up in the South, the North, the East or the West. So, they packed fur parkas, tennis shorts, ski boots, sandals, ear muffs and swim suits, and so forth and so on. Just guessing, Max speculated that their baggage weighed seven tons. As a result, they left it where it was—in the living room, kitchen, up the stairs, and in the bedroom—tossed a change of underwear into a manila envelope and left for the train station.

They had no trouble locating the train once they reached the station. It had both a number—one-thousand-four-hundred-seventy-six—and a name—The Miami Beach Local.

"Doesn't this train go to New York?" Max asked the conductor as he and 99 climbed aboard.

"That's right—it doesn't," the conductor, a fat, jol-

ly-looking man with a white beard, replied. "We're still
on the winter schedule. All trains—including New
York trains—go to Miami Beach."

"That's the first thing about this case that's made
sense," Max said to 99, leading the way along the corridor to their compartment. "You know who ought to
be running this country? The same people who manage
the railroads. There's an old saying: What's good for
the St. Louis, Lackawana, St. Pierre & Hudson is good
for the St. Louis, Lackawana, St. Pierre & Hudson."
He opened the door to the compartment and looked
in, then entered, motioning for 99 to follow. "These
modern trains are certainly much different from the
old ones," he said approvingly, looking around. "Look
—we have our own private coal stove."

"It's very nice," 99 said. "But, Max, I think we
ought to start looking for that contingent of KAOS assassins while passengers are still boarding."

Max looked at her coolly. "99, I'll make the decisions," he said. "Not only do I have seniority, but I'm
head of the family. And, you are all wrong when you
say that passengers are still boarding the train."

"I am, Max?"

"People are boarding the train," Max explained.
"They don't become passengers until after they're on
board. See how wrong you were? Will you just let me
make the command decisions from now on?"

"Yes, Max."

"Fine. Now, let's go start looking for that contingent
of KAOS assassins while *people* are still boarding.
And, while we're doing it, we can also look over the
passengers who are already aboard."

Max and 99 left the compartment and began stroll-
ing along the aisle, sizing up the people who were
boarding and the passengers who were already aboard.

"Be casual," Max said to 99. "Make it look as if

we're simply out for a morning constitutional. It's too bad we didn't think to bring along a dog to walk."

"I'm being casual, Max," 99 said. "You're the one who looks nervous."

"I can't help it," Max replied. "I think, down deep, I have a guilty conscience about spying. My real philosophy is: what other people do is none of my business." He held out a hand. "See? I'm shaking like a leaf. Let's start jogging, 99, so we won't be so conspicuous."

"Jogging? Not conspicuous?"

"Everybody jogs these days, 99. But how many people amble up and down the aisle of a train looking for KAOS assassins? If I could only——" He suddenly brightened. "I've got it!" To calm himself, he got the Coolidge-head penny from his pocket, and casually flipped it into the air, then caught it, as they proceeded along the aisle.

"Max," 99 complained, "now you're making *me* nervous. I'm afraid you'll lose that penny. It's the only way we'll have of contacting Control once we find out where the KAOS meeting is being held, you know. Without that penny, the whole mission might abort."

"99, relax," Max replied reassuringly. "Flipping a coin is as natural to me as eating or sleeping or crossing my toes. I do it without thinking. And, as far as I know, I never miss."

"Sir!" a voice called.

Max and 99 stopped and looked back. A large, fat, evil-looking man wearing dark glasses was gesturing to Max. "I believe this is yours," he said. He returned to where Max and 99 were standing and put the Coolidge-head penny into Max's open hand. "You dropped it as I was passing you," the man said. Then he turned and continued along the aisle.

"Max . . . what was that you were saying?" 99 said.

"Well . . . maybe I miss every once in a while," Max replied. "But in the long run—"

"Not that," 99 said. "I mean about crossing your toes. Max, that's not natural. I've never heard of anybody who could cross their toes before. Max . . . why didn't you tell me about this *before* we were married?"

"I'm sorry, 99," Max replied. "I just didn't think it was worth mentioning. It comes natural to me, so I thought it was natural for everybody—as natural as being double-jointed."

"Well . . . a lot of people have double-jointed fingers, that's true," 99 said.

"Fingers? I'm talking about double-jointed eyelids. Don't tell me *that* isn't natural, either! I'm beginning to won—" Max abruptly interrupted himself, looking thoughtful. "99—that big, fat, evil-looking fellow with the dark glasses. Isn't that a lot like what a typical KAOS assassin would look like?"

"Max, I think you're right!" 99 looked up the aisle. "Do you see him? Where did he go?"

"I don't see him at the moment," Max replied. "But we know the direction he took—he went forward. And if you go forward on a train, the only other way you can go is backwards. You can't turn left, and you can't turn right. And we know he didn't come back this way. So, if he didn't stop going forward and reverse his direction and come back this way, then he must be— I'll tell you what, 99. Let's just stand right here. Maybe he'll pass by again."

99 pointed forward. "All we have to do is go that way—the way *he* went—Max."

Max shrugged. "Frankly, it sounds too simple to me. But, I'll humor you, 99. We'll go that way."

Max and 99 started forward, intending to track down the big, fat, evil-looking man in the dark glasses. At that same instant, however, the train began pulling out—and it started with such a jolt that Max and 99 lost their balance and stumbled backwards through seven cars, ending up on the rear observation platform.

"99! Are you all right?"

"Yes, Max," 99 replied, rising. "How about you?"

Max got to his feet. "I'm not sure yet," he said. He grimaced, as if exerting great effort. "Yes . . . okay down there—my toes still cross," he reported.

"Is it *that* difficult, Max?"

"Only when I'm wearing shoes," he replied. He blinked rapidly. "Yes, I'm okay all over, 99," he said. "The old eyelids still bend both ways. Now—where were we?"

"On the trail of the big, fat, evil-looking man with the dark glasses," 99 replied. "Let's go, Max!"

"Fine. And . . . ah, on the way, 99 . . . ah, would you keep an eye out for a Coolidge-head penny, please. . . . When the train started, I was yanked right out from under it. It was in mid-flip and—Well, you get the picture."

"Oh, Max!"

Proceeding slowly, looking into every nook and cranny for the Coolidge-head penny, Max and 99 made their way forward. When they reached the car they had been in when the train started, they found the fat, jolly-looking conductor with the white beard standing in the aisle examining something small in his hand and chuckling.

"Ah . . . I wonder . . ." Max said. "Is that, by any chance, a Coolidge-head penny?"

The conductor looked disappointed. "Oh, so that's what it is," he said. "I guess I was holding it upside down. I thought it was a Lincoln-head penny and Lincoln was wearing a false beard." He handed the penny to Max.

"A beard that looks like an upside-down Indian head-dress?" Max said.

"Lincoln was a great humorist, you know," the conductor explained. Then he moved on down the aisle. "Tickets!" he called. "Have your tickets ready!"

Again, Max and 99 moved forward. As before, Max flipped the penny to keep cool. And, once more, watching him flip it, 99 grew increasingly apprehensive.

A short while later, they reached the lounge car. There, at the far end, they spotted the big, fat, evil-looking man in the dark glasses. He was seated in a lounge chair and surrounded by nearly a dozen other evil-looking men in dark glasses—some fat, some thin and some just right. The object of their chase seemed to be holding court. One or another of the men would speak to him, then he would reply. And when he was talking all the others remained silent and attentive.

"Well, is there any doubt in your mind who the big, fat man in the dark glasses is, 99?" Max said. "That's Arbuthnot. He's the Great Teacher. And those are his students. I think we've found the location of the meeting. It's being held right here on this train. Now, I'll just rub this Coolidge-head penny and we'll—"

"Max," 99 broke in, "don't you think we ought to be a little more positive before we have the Chief send a squad of Control agents to take these men into custody? Suppose that *isn't* Arbuthnot? And suppose those aren't—"

"All right, 99" Max said. "I have never been so sure of anything in my life. But, since, technically, I suppose, we're still on our honeymoon and I'm humoring you, I'll squander a little time and prove to you that I'm right. Now—see those two empty chairs near that group of men? Well, you and I will saunter over there and then we'll occupy those seats and we'll eavesdrop on the conversation. Okay?"

"Yes, Max."

99 sauntered to the far end of the car and then sat down in one of the unoccupied chairs near the group

of men that Max had identified as KAOS assassins. When she was seated, Max, still flipping the coin, moved toward her. He had taken only one step, however, when he missed the Coolidge-head penny and it fell in the aisle and then rolled under a chair that was occupied by a little old white-haired lady.

Max got down on his hands and knees and peered under the chair. The little old lady, misunderstanding, whacked him on the back of the head with her purse.

"I'm sorry, mam," Max apologized, rising and rubbing the back of his head, "but I lost a valuable coin under your chair. I wonder if you would mind getting up for a minute?"

The little old lady cupped a hand around an ear. "What's that you just lied to me?" she shouted. "I don't hear good."

Max glanced around. The lounge car was crowded and everyone was staring at him. He faced back to the little old lady. "I said I lost a penny under your seat!" he told her, speaking loudly. "Would you stand up?"

"I can't stand the heat, either!" she shouted. "But it's not hot enough in here to make a big, strappin' boy like you go faint and fall in the aisle. Get along with you, now, or I'll break open your skull with my purse and let the sawdust fall out!"

"You may have that purse full of sawdust, but it certainly didn't feel like it when you hit me," Max shouted back. "And if you use it on me once more, I'll kick you right in the shins—I don't care if you are a hard-of-hearing old hen with white hair!"

The little old lady smiled apologetically. "Why didn't you say you dropped a penny under my chair," she chided. "Go ahead and get it—I don't mind."

"Thank you," Max said.

As soon as he had retrieved the Coolidge-head penny, Max joined 99, seating himself beside her and near the alleged KAOS assassins.

"No matter how it turns out otherwise, this trip is a success for me already," he whispered to 99. "I finally found out how to handle little old white-haired ladies. You have to threaten to kick them in the shins." He glanced toward the group of men in dark glasses. "Are you convinced yet?" he asked.

"Not exactly, Max," 99 replied. "Listen to what they're saying."

Max leaned toward the group of men.

"Sir," one of the thin, evil-looking men said to the big, fat evil-looking man, "all the yo-yo industry wants to do is make the men in the Army happy. We don't care anything about selling yo-yos. We'd be happy to give these yo-yos to the men in the armed services, except that if we didn't make a profit, we couldn't pay our taxes, could we? And if we didn't pay our taxes, where would the government get the money to pay the men in the armed services? So, do you see what I'm getting at?"

"Well . . . 'round-about, yeah," the big' fat, evil-looking man replied. "But 'splain it to me, anyways."

"All the yo-yo industry wants you to do—as Chairman of the Committee on Army Purchasing—is to pressure the Chief of Staff to buy our yo-yos for three-hundred dollars a dozen. That way, we'll make a bigger profit, and—if we're caught—we'll pay higher taxes, and, unless it's used for something else, like raising Senators' salaries, there will be more money to pay the men in the armed services. Get it?"

"I don't know—*do* I get it?" the big, fat, evil-looking man asked. "And, if I do, what percentage?"

"Ten per cent, sir?"

"That's fine. Just send the check to my favorite charity—the Society for the Preservation of the Coonskin Cap. Make it out to my wife—she's the head coonskin."

"Yes, sir!"

"Sir," another thin, evil-looking man said, "we in the skinless frankfurter business have an old saying. It goes: What's good for the yo-yo industry is good for the skinless frankfurter industry. Now, keeping that in mind . . ."

Max leaned back toward 99. "Are you convinced?" he asked. "Shall I rub the Coolidge-head penny now?"

"Max! Those aren't KAOS assassins! After hearing that conversation, don't you know who they are? That big, fat, evil-looking man in the dark glasses is a senator. And all those other evil-looking men in dark glasses are lobbyists."

Max glanced again toward the group. "You mean men who try to get senators and representatives and other people in government to do special favors for them?" he said. He turned back to 99. "That's terrible! I didn't think they were serious." He shook his head. "I find that hard to believe, 99 He doesn't look like a senator to me."

"Of course not, Max—he's wearing dark glasses. But, if you don't believe me, ask him."

"I will," Max said. He moved his chair closer to the group, then broke in on the conversation. "Excuse me, sir," he said, addressing the big, fat, evil-looking man, "but my wife and I are having a disagreement—"

"Bring it around when it's born, and I'll kiss it on the forehead," the fat man said. "That's the worst thing about being a statesman—all that baby-kissing."

"No, I mean we have a difference of opinion. You see, I think you're Arbuthnot, the international assassin and Great Teacher, and my wife thinks you're just another corrupt politician. Which one of us is correct?"

"You're both wrong," the big, fat, evil-looking man replied. "I'm not 'just another' corrupt politician. Why, I'm famous from coast to coast and border to border for my corruptionness."

"Oh . . . well, I guess that answers my question," Max said. "I'm sorry I slighted you by calling you 'just another' corrupt politician. Are you on Senate business now?"

"Yup. I'm headin' down to Miami Beach to investigate all them terrible slum conditions in New York City," the big, fat, evil-looking man replied.

"But, New York City is up North," Max pointed out.

"I know that," the Senator said. "But, what can I do? South is the way the train's headed."

Max moved his chair back to where it was before. "You're wrong, 99," he said. "That's not Arbuthnot, the international assassin, it's just another corrupt politician."

"Max, that's what *I* said. You're the one who said it was Arbuthnot."

"All right, 99—if that's what you want to believe. I'm still humoring you, so anything you say—I agree. Now, let's try to concentrate on the mission again, shall we? Look around the lounge car—do you see anybody who looks like a KAOS assassin?"

"I looked while you were talking to the Senator, Max," 99 said. "I couldn't find anyone who looked suspicious. Let's stroll up and down the aisle again."

"That's very romantic, 99. But, don't you— Oh, I see what you mean. And look for suspicious-looking characters, you mean."

Max and 99 rose and left the lounge car and sauntered toward the rear of the train. Several cars later, they suddenly saw a herd of burly girls marching toward them. The girls looked a great deal like lady wrestlers.

"Back!" Max shouted to 99. "Flatten yourself against the wall! It's a stampede! We could be crushed!"

There was a thundering sound as the burly girls

drew nearer. Max and 99 pressed themselves against
the wall. But they could not possibly flatten themselves
out enough, and it seemed as if they would surely be
crushed to pulp as the burly girls rumbled past. But, in
the nick of time, the wall suddenly appeared to give
'way. Max and 99 stumbled backwards, out of the
way, and the burly girls thundered by them, leaving
behind a cloud of dust from the carpet in the aisle.

"That was close!" Max said. "What saved us?"

"The door opened and we fell into this vacant compartment, Max," 99 explained.

"Oh . . . yes . . ." Max looked around, "Mmmmmm
. . . that's odd, isn't it? The train is crowded . . . yet we
have this vacant compartment. Do you suppose it's being
used by someone who doesn't want it known that he's
on the train?"

"Max, I don't quite understand your reasoning . . ."

"Sometimes, 99, an experienced secret agent gets a
hunch. He can't explain it, but— You'll notice, for instance, that there's no luggage in this compartment.
That makes it *seem* vacant. And yet, a closer look re-
veals this manila envelope, which contains—" Max
opened the envelope and was peering into it. "—which
contains—" He closed the envelope and dropped it
onto the seat. "Nevermind, 99, you were wrong
again," he said. "If you'd looked on the door before
we fell in here, you'd have noticed that this is our own
compartment. Let's get back to—"

From the aisle came the voice of the conductor.
"Lunch! Lunch is now being served in the Dining Car!
Lunch! Hear ye! Hear—"

Once more, the sound of a stampede was heard.
The conductor leaped into Max's and 99's compartment, getting out of the way. A great mass of people
suddenly galloped past the doorway. Then, just as
abruptly, all became quiet once more—except for the
sound of the dust settling.

"What was that!" Max asked the conductor.

"Just the folks going in to lunch," he replied. "They all want to be first in line."

"It looked like everybody on the train went past," Max said.

"They did," the conductor said. "I guess I better get up to the dining car and set the table." He hurried out and then disappeared up the aisle.

"Well, now we know who the KAOS assassins are, 99," Max said.

She looked puzzled. "We do, Max?"

"Of course. Didn't you notice when that thundering herd went by that those big girls with those big muscles weren't with them? That could mean only one thing!"

"That they were in the powder room when lunch was announced, you mean?"

"What I should have said, perhaps, is that it could mean only one of *two* things. The other one—the right one—is that they're the KAOS assassins. Think about it, 99. Were those *really* big girls with big muscles, or were they actually big *men* with big muscles? Now, if they were men, isn't it reasonable to assume that they're the KAOS assassins in disguise?"

"I guess that *is* kind of reasonable to assume, Max," 99 admitted. "But, frankly, they looked like girls to me."

"99, I suspect I've had a great deal more experience at girl-watching than you. And I say they looked like men."

"Max . . . I'm hungry. Let's go to lunch and argue about it."

"Good idea."

Max and 99 left the compartment and walked along the aisle in the direction the conductor had gone. When they reached the last car they saw the end of a line up ahead.

Max looked back. "I wonder where those men with the big muscles are?" he said, sounding a little worried. "If they're KAOS assassins, they might be up to anything."

Max and 99 got in line.

"My guess is, they're girls and they're on a diet and they're skipping lunch," 99 said.

"99, I think I know—"

The sound of marching was heard again.

"Here they come," Max said, relieved.

A moment later, the burly girls marched into the car and got in line behind Max and 99.

"If those aren't KAOS assassins in disguise," Max whispered to 99, "my number isn't 86. I'm going to try to get them to make a slip and reveal their true identities." He then turned to the burly girl who was standing in line right behind him and who appeared to be the leader. "Well . . . nice train ride we're having," he said cordially. "Which is quite a surprise, considering how crowded it is. You'd think there'd be chaos, eh?"

"Not for us," the burly girl replied. "Everybody gets out of our way."

"I see. Well, that means it's chaos for everybody else, then, when you're around. Is that right?"

The burly girl eyed him belligerently. "You trying to get fresh, puny?"

"Puny. Uh . . . no, I was, uh, just, uh . . . Well, uh, on your way to Miami Beach on vacation, are you?" Max asked.

"Business," the leader of the burly girls replied. "We're a team of lady wrestlers. We're going down to Miami Beach to break some legs on some other lady wrestlers."

Max faced back to 99. "A likely story," he whispered. "They're a team, all right—but a team of KAOS assassins, not a team of lady wrestlers."

"Max . . . they *look* like lady wrestlers," 99 said.

"Of course. That's the dead-giveaway. They wouldn't look like assassins, would they? If they looked like assassins, we'd be able to spot them as assassins immediately. KAOS isn't in the business of making things easy for Control, you know, 99. Now, watch this. With a couple deft verbal parries and thrusts, I'll trick this assassin into revealing not only that he's not a wrestler, but that also he's not a lady."

"Be careful, Max," 99 said worriedly.

Max turned back to the leader of the burly girls. "Frankly," he said, "I don't happen to believe that you're either a lady or—"

Max found himself sailing through the air, headed for the opposite end of the car. The burly girl, upon having her word questioned, had picked him up, held him over her head a moment, then sent him flying. A moment later, Max crashed against the door at the end of the car and with the usual thud, dropped to the floor.

"Max!" 99 cried, running to him. "Are you all right?"

Max shook his head groggily to clear his vision. "I probably won't know whether I'm all right or not until after I see the X-rays," he replied. "In the meantime, however, I think I've proved at least half of my suspicion. That fellow may be a wrestler, all right, but he's certainly no lady!" With 99's help, he got to his feet. "I think I'll wait until after lunch before I prove the other half, though," he said. "The next time I get thrown against that door, I want to have more padding inside me. I hope they're serving something light and fluffy for lunch."

Max and 99 returned to the line, which had become considerably shorter. As they approached, the burly girls steps back so that they could resume their place.

"No, you go ahead," Max said to the burly girls.

"You know the old saying: Lady wrestlers first, if you don't want your arm twisted."

The burly girls accepted Max's gentlemanly gesture. One by one, they began entering the dining car. As the second from the last entered the car and the door closed behind her, Max turned to 99, looking puzzled. "Did you see that?" he said. "I caught a glimpse of the inside of the dining car when the door was open and it looked like a corn field."

"Max, don't be silly."

"Just watch," Max said.

The door to the dining car opened and the last of the burly girls entered. Then the door quickly closed.

"Max, you're right!" 99 said. "Only it doesn't look like a field of corn. It looks like a pasture—with Jersey cows!"

"99—I have a theory."

"What is it, Max?"

"Do you suppose those cows ate that corn?"

"Max, I don't think that's the most important—"

"The sheep couldn't have done it, you know. The sheep are in the meadow. It's the cows who are always in the corn. At least, according to the story I heard. Remember that story, 99? The sheep are in the meadow, the cows are in the corn, Little Bo Peep is fast asleep under the curds and whey, while Jack be Nimble—"

"Max! The important thing is, I think we better find out what's behind that door!"

"You're probably right, 99," Max replied. Cautiously, he got hold of the doorknob. "Stand back," he said. "I'm going to open it." He turned the knob, then pulled. But the door remained closed. "It won't open," Max reported, puzzled. He released the knob.

Just then, the door opened by itself. Instead of entering the dining car, though, Max —who was next in line—stayed where he was. He and 99 looked past the open doorway. What they saw, rather than the inside of a dining car, was scenery. A meadow, a farm house, then a pond flashed by. A moment later, the door closed automatically.

"That explains it!" 99 said, impressed.

"It certainly does," Max nodded. He turned to 99. "You tell me your idea of how it explains it, then I'll tell you mine," he said.

"Don't you see, Max? That door to the dining car is operated by some sort of electronic timer. It lets in one passenger at a time. But, actually, the door opens into space. The passengers didn't enter a dining car, they stepped off the train—to their deaths!"

"Exactly the way I had it figured out, Max said approvingly.

"What should we do, Max?"

"I think we better find that conductor," Max replied. "He'll probably want to put a warning sign on this door."

99 looked back along the aisle. "Max . . . we seem to be the only passengers left."

"I know that, 99. That's why I want a sign on that door. We could get killed going to dinner this evening if something isn't done about the dining car!"

3.

MAX AND 99 LOCATED THE CONDUCTOR—the fat, jolly-looking man with the white beard—a short while later. He was in the lounge car alone, standing behind the soda fountain, mixing himself a chocolate soda. The conductor looked quite surprised when he saw Max and 99 enter the car and approach the soda fountain.

"We'd like to report an accident," Max said.

"I can see it," the conductor replied. "How come you two didn't step off the train—to your deaths—with all the others?"

"No, no, that's not the accident," Max said. "The accident is that the door to the dining car— Oh, you know—" He peered at the conductor narrowly. "If you *know* about it," he said, "Then apparently it wasn't an accident—it was planned. And the only people I know who would plan a mass assassination are—"

The fat, jolly-looking, bearded conductor had produced a pistol from behind the soda fountain and was pointing it at Max and 99. "And the only person I know who would know that the only people he knew who would plan a mass assassination would be a Control agent," he said. With the pistol, he gestured toward the front of the train. "March!" he ordered. "All the way to the eingine!"

Max and 99 made their way up the aisle, with the conductor following them, keeping his gun pointed at them.

"Keep an eye out for a guy with feathers," Max whispered to 99. "He'll be the injun."

"Not injun, Max. Engine."

"Oh. I guess that does make a lot more sense. After all, we're on a train, not a reservation. Although . . . we have a compartment. And you can't get a compartment without a reservation." He looked thoughtful. "Just to be on the safe side, 99, keep an eye out for a guy with feathers, anyway."

"All right, Max."

They soon reached the engine. It was not easy to enter, however. More than a dozen men were crowded into a small space that normally accomodated only the engineer and the fireman.

"Coming through!" the conductor shouted. "Watch it! Coming through with Control agent prisoners!"

The men cleared a small passageway and Max and 99 and the conductor squeezed past, then reached a small, wispy, saucer-eyed, nervous-looking man who was seated at the controls of the train.

"Arbuthnot," the conductor said to the man, "look what I caught!" He seemed proud.

Arbuthnot, KAOS's master assassin, looked at Max and 99 and screamed. "Control agents! Get them out of here! Control agents have germs!" He then fainted.

"Wheeeee!" the man standing behind Arbuthnot shouted. "Now, it's my turn." He shoved Arbuthnot out of the seat and took his place at the controls.

"Give me a hand here," the conductor said to Max and 99. "You two pick him up and carry him back to the lounge car. He looks like he needs a good stiff chocolate soda."

"You said 'give you a hand'," Max replied. "What are *you* going to be doing?"

"Somebody has to carry the gun," the conductor pointed out.

Max and 99 picked up Arbuthnot, who weighed not much more than a feather pillow, and maneuvered him out of the crowded engine, then headed back down the aisle with him toward the lunge car.

"Those men in the engine—" Max said to the conductor. "Were they, by any chance, a contingent of KAOS assassins on the way to a secret siminar?"

"That's Classified information," the conductor replied.

"How about this, then?" Max said. "What are all those KAOS assassins who are on their way to a secret seminar doing up there in the engine? Is that Classified?"

"Oh, no—I can tell you that," the conductor replied. "When we were planning this trip, we voted on whether to travel by stolen plane or stolen train. Well, stolen train won by a wide margin. Almost all of us, we discovered, had a secret hankering to drive a train. I was the only one who didn't—and I had a secret hankering to take tickets on a train and walk up and down the aisle calling 'Lunch is now being served in the dining car.' So, we hijacked this train to take us to the secret meeting place. That's why all those KAOS assassins who are on their way to a secret seminar are up there in the engine. They're playing engineer. Scratch a ruthless, hardbitten KAOS assassin, and, every time, you'll find a cutesy-pie little kid underneath."

"Assassinating all the other passengers—I suppose that was a kid trick, too!" 99 said.

"Are you kidding?" the conductor replied, hurt.

"The way that was done? That had real technique—it was professional. A kid would've just gone through the cars with a machine gun, blasting away. It would've been fun, sure. But no technique."

"He's right, 99," Max said. "There was certainly nothing amateurish about the way he wiped out those passengers. I think you owe him an apology."

"Sorry . . ." 99 said.

They had reached the lounge car. Max and 99 put Arbuthnot in a chair. The the conductor mixed a chocolate soda—straight—and waved it under the master assassin's nose. He stirred. His eyes opened. After a sip of the chocolate soda he regained full consciousness. But when he saw Max and 99 he looked as if he were going to faint again.

"Get away!" he shrieked at Max and 99. "I don't want your Control germs!"

The conductor took Max and 99 to the far end of the car. "Stay right here," he ordered. "Arbuthnot's got a thing about germs. He's a regular nut on the subject. You ought to see him when he starts out on an assignment to assassinate somebody. He puts on a face mask and rubber gloves and sterilizes his gun or knife or poison—as the case may be—and—"

"Come back here!" Arbuthnot called to the conductor. "Do you want to catch something!"

The conductor left Max and 99 at the end of the car and walked back to where Arbuthnot was seated.

"Well," Arbuthnot called to Max and 99, "so you were sent by Control to follow us and locate our secret meeting place, were you?"

"Sorry," Max shouted back, "but that's Classified information."

"Which?" Arbuthnot asked. "That you were sent by Control? Or that you were sent to locate our secret meeting place?"

"Both," Max replied.

"Shall I take them to lunch in the dining car?" the conductor asked Arbuthnot.

"No—we'll keep them alive," Arbuthnot replied. "We'll use them as hostages in case Control happens to find out where we're holding our secret meeting. When we get—"

The train suddenly jerked to a halt. Max and 99 were thrown against the end of the car, and Arbuthnot and the conductor were hurled down the aisle and ended up in a tangle with Max and 99.

"Get me out of this!" Arbuthnot screeched. "I'm getting their germs all over me! Ugh! In panic, he scrambled out of the tangle, then raced to the other end of the car and huddled in a corner. There, crouching, he got out a spray bottle and began spraying the surrounding air and himself with disinfectant.

Max and 99 were so fascinated by Arbuthnot's performance that they made no effort to try to escape. As a result, the conductor was able to disentangle himself and get the drop on them again.

The train began moving once more.

"Well . . . that went pretty smoothly," the conductor said, pleased.

"Smoothly?" Max said. "That was the roughest whatever-it-was I've ever experienced. What was it?"

"We just switched from the main track to a side track," the conductor replied. "The side track will take us to the secret meeting place. Nobody will know where we are."

"I doubt that," Max said. "Won't the railroad miss the train when it doesn't arrive at its destination?"

"They'll just think it's late," the conductor replied. "Who ever heard of a train arriving at its destination on time?"

"You're probably right about that," Max admitted. "But the place this track takes the train to—won't the people there be a little suspicious of a train that arrives with only two passengers and a crew of fumblethumbs running it?"

The conductor grinned broadly. "Boy, are you in for a surprise!" he said.

Again, the train suddenly halted. Max and 99 and the conductor were thrown against the end of the car once more. Arbuthnot, however, flattened himself in the aisle this time, avoiding being hurled the length of the car.

"All out for Los Angeles!" the conductor shouted, rising. "End of the line! All out for Los Angeles!"

"Los Angeles?" 99 said doubtfully, as she and Max got to their feet. "You mean we traveled all the way across the country in that short time? I don't believe it."

"Not *that* Los Angeles," the conductor explained. "This is the other Los Angeles."

"Get them out of here!" Arbuthnot bellowed from the other end of the car. "I want to fumigate the place!"

The conductor gestured to Max and 99 with his pistol. As they left the car, they saw Arbuthnot beginning to spray the interior with the disinfectant.

"Max! Look!" 99 said, as they stepped down from the car. "It's— It's— It's a ghost town!"

"Yes," Max said, looking around at the deserted streets and ramshackle buildings. He turned to the conductor. "Well, you were certainly right—I am surprised. Where are we?"

"I told you—this is the other Los Angeles," the conductor replied. "This, in fact, is the original. A bunch of people from Iowa and Nebraska settled here a long time ago and named the place Los Angeles. But they found out they were too far from the freeways, so they moved out west and took the name with them." He chuckled. "But, the joke was on them," he continued. "They found out when they got out there that they couldn't get their covered wagons onto the free-ways, anyway. The car traffic was too heavy—you know?"

Arbuthnot appeared in the doorway of the car. He looked down at the dusty street. "Eeeeeek!" he screeched. He tossed the spray bottle to the conductor. "Disinfect it!" he commanded.

The conductor sprayed the dust. Then he started to toss the spray bottle back to Arbuthnot.

"Wait!" Arbuthnot shouted. "It's covered with your germs!" he said. He got out another spray bottle and lobbed it to the conductor. "Disinfect it first," he ordered.

The conductor sprayed the first spray bottle with spray from the second spray bottle, then tossed it to Arbuthnot. He kept the second spray bottle because by then, of course, it was loaded with germs.

"I won't set a foot in that filthy place until it's sprayed," Arbuthnot said. "Take the prisoners with you and disinfect the whole town. When you're finished, signal, and we'll all meet at the saloon."

Max and 99 were marched off by the conductor. They met the other assassins, who were descending from the engine. Then, from the baggage car, the conductor got a case of spray bottles. He handed them out and the assassins dispersed and began disinfecting the buildings and the streets.

The conductor put Max and 99 to work spraying the hotel, while he followed along behind, holding his pistol on them. They disinfected the lobby, then the dining room, then the kitchen. After that, they went upstairs and disinfected all the bedrooms. Then they left the hotel and crossed the street to the saloon. The other assassins, save for one, were waiting for them.

"Where's Fred?" the conductor asked.

No one knew.

"Oh, well, he'll be along," the conductor said. He

raised his pistol and fired a shot, signalling to Arbuthnot.

From overhead there was a scream.

"That was Fred," one of the assassins said. "I forgot
—he said he was going up to spray the roof."

The conductor frowned. "I wonder how that'll read
on my record?" he said. "Is it a plus or a minus if you
assassinate one of your own men?"

That started a discussion among the assassins. But it
was interrupted a few minutes later by the arrival of
Arbuthnot.

"Spray the prisoners again," Arbuthnot ordered
from the doorway.

The conductor disinfected Max and 99 once more.

Arbuthnot sniffed the air. "Good," he said. "Not a
living germ within miles, now." He entered the saloon
and began looking around. There was a long bar with
a long mirror behind it and a number of tables and
chairs. The walls were elaborately panelled. The floor
was made of wide planks that had large cracks between them.

As Arbuthnot inspected the premises, the other assassins watched him closely, waiting for his judgment.
The conductor kept the spray bottle poised, ready to
disinfect anything that might elicit his displeasure. Max
and 99 stood apart from the others.

"Now, Max," 99 whispered. "Rub the Coolidge-
head penny and signal our location to the Chief."

"Not yet, 99," Max whispered back. "That may be
exactly what Arbuthnot wants. This could be a trick.
Don't forget—the conductor recognized us instantly as
Control agents—it's possible that he knew all along
that we were on the train. And if he knew that, maybe
he knows about the plan to signal the location of the
meeting to the Chief. For all we know, Arbuthnot ordered this stop at this ghost town for our benefit. Perhaps he wants us to signal the Chief, and, after we do,

he'll move on to some other location. We're not deal-
ing with a common-ordinary bad guy, 99. Arbuthnot is
brilliant. A kook, yes—but brilliant."

"Max," 99 whispered, "I think you're giving him too
much credit. How could he possibly know about the
Coolidge-head penny?"

"I didn't say he knows about the penny, 99. I said
he may know that we're going to signal. He may be
waiting for us to make our move and reveal our
method. So, as soon as I can attract his attention, I'm
going to flip the penny. And if he tries to get it from
me, I'll rub it quickly and alert the Chief to our where-
abouts."

"Max," 99 said worriedly, "I think that's—"

But Arbuthnot had finished his inspection. "Well,
it's not the Grand Forks, North Dakota, Hilton," he
said, "but, on the other hand, we won't have a lot of
strangers wandering in and out of the lobby and
breathing their germs on us. We ought to be able to
get a lot of work done." He indicated Max and 99.
"Put them away somewhere for safe-keeping," he said
to the conductor.

"Just a minute," Max said, getting the Coolidge-
head penny from his pocket. "As one of the abductees
in this arrangement, I would like—"

"One of the whats?" Arbuthnot asked.

"Abductees," Max replied. "You and your fellow
assassins are the abductors and we are the abductees."
He flipped the penny and caught it. "As one of the abductees—" Again, he flipped the coin and caught it.
"Yes? Did you want to interrupt me for something?"
he asked Arbuthnot.

Arbuthnot shook his head.

"As one of the abductees—" Max continued. He
flipped the penny and snatched it from the air once
more. "Did you mention something about an interest
in odd coins?" he asked.

"Not me," Arbuthnot replied. "I never go near them. Odd coins have odd germs." He addressed the conductor again. "Get them out of here," he said.

"This is your final chance," Max said. He flipped the penny into the air again.

"Max!" 99 hissed. "Stop flipping that penny and—"

He turned to her. "What did you say, 99? I was busy flipping the—"

There was a clink. Max had failed to catch the penny and it had dropped to the floor.

"Max!"

The Coolidge-head penny was rolling across the floor. Max dashed after it.

But just then, Arbuthnot shouted, "Spray it! He was handling it—it's germ-infested!"

And as Max was about to reach the penny, the conductor sprayed. The spray missed the coin and hit Max straight in the face. And the Coolidge-head penny got away and rolled down a crack between two planks.

"Max! It's gone!" 99 cried.

Max was wiping spray from his face. "Gone where?" he replied, on the brink of panic.

"All this excitement about a penny?" Arbuthnot asked. "You people in Control sure must be poorly-paid." He spoke to the conductor again. "Get them out of here!" he said.

"Just let me get that penny!" Max protested. "Where did it go?"

"It's too late, Max!" 99 told him. "It dropped through the floor."

"Oh," Max replied, looking pained. He thought a second, then spoke to Arbuthnot. "I wonder if I could borrow a few of your assassins for a minute to help me pull up these planks," he said.

"Enough!" Arbuthnot screeched. He turned to the conductor, "Take care of him!" he commanded.

The conductor dug into his pocket, got out some

change, and handed a penny to Max. "There—now, we're square," he said.

"That's not what I meant!" Arbuthnot screamed. "You're an assassin, not a banker! When I say 'take care of him,' I mean— Oh, nevermind. Just get them out of here! All this commotion is stirring up the germs!"

4.

THE CONDUCTOR MOTIONED to Max and 99, directing them outside. When they reached the street, he ordered them to halt. Then he glanced about, looking for a place to imprison them.

"How about putting us back on the train," Max suggested. "You could lock us in the baggage car."

"If it's your idea, it couldn't be any good," the conductor replied.

"Why don't you lock us in a room in the hotel," 99 suggested.

The conductor looked shocked.

"It's all right—we're married," 99 assured him.

The conductor looked suspicious. "Yeah? That's what they all say. Let's see your marriage license."

"I don't carry it with me," Max said. "But, use your head—why would we want to be locked in the same hotel room if we weren't married?"

The conductor thought for a moment. "I don't know," he said finally. "But, you're so anxious, there must be something you could do. And you're not going to use me for your patsy. I'll think of someplace else to lock you up. There must be—" He suddenly brightened. "Sure! There's always an abandoned mine in these old ghost towns." He shaded his eyes and squinted toward the hills. "It's up there somewhere," he said. He motioned with the pistol again. "March!"

Max, 99 and the conductor left the town and walked to the foothills. After a short search, the conductor located the entrance to an abandoned mine.

"See? I knew it would be here," he said. "You watch educational TV and you learn a lot of things."

"Oh? What did you see this on?" Max asked. " 'Abandoned Mines and Other Curious Natural Phenomena'?"

The conductor shook his head. "In a movie," he replied. " 'Abbott & Costello Meet Wolf Man on the Planet of the Ants.' It was about this beautiful girl who was engaged to marry the local banker's son because her father couldn't keep up the mortgage payments on his Dairy Queen stand. Abbott was masquerading as the girl, and Costello was chasing him across the ice, assisted by a pack of ravenous ants, when suddenly the ice broke and they dropped into this abandoned mine. I remember it because, although they were supposed to be shooting the picture on location in Antarctica, I kept catching glimpses of a sign saying 'Los Angeles City Limits,' and we're in Los Angeles now, aren't we?"

"You're right," Max replied. "You watch educational TV and you learn a lot of things."

Again, the conductor gestured with the gun. "Inside!" he said.

"Have you noticed," Max said, "that there's no door on this abandoned mine? How do you intend to lock us in?"

"A rock slide," the conductor replied. "That's how it was done in 'Abbott & Costello Meet—' Nevermind. Just watch—I'll show you."

Max and 99 entered the abandoned mine. Then the conductor pointed his pistol into the air and fired it. There was a loud rumbling noise. A moment later, rocks came crashing down and completely covered the entrance to the abandoned mine, leaving Max and 99 trapped inside in total darkness.

"That's how," the conductor called in to them. "It has something to do with sound waves, I think. Either that or I'm magic."

"Sound waves is my guess," Max shouted back. "But how are you going to open that rock slide when it's time to feed us?"

"Sound waves," the conductor replied.

"That only works one way," Max called out to him.

"I guess you better start hoping you were wrong about me not being magic, then," the conductor said. "See you later—maybe."

"Wait!" Max cried.

There was no response.

"He's gone, Max," 99 said dismally. "What are we going to do now?"

"Don't panic, 99," Max said calmly. "As I see it, we have several choices. We can use sound waves. Or we can use magic. Or we can die a horrible death. Now, as for the use of sound waves— Or, on the other hand, magic can be— Isn't it funny, 99, how the first reaction so often turns out to be the correct reaction? You were right to panic."

"If we only had a light—" 99 said. "I can't see a thing. But this mine tunnel must lead somewhere. Why don't we try following it in the dark, Max?"

"Because we'd lose it," Max replied. "You know how impossible it is to shadow in the dark, 99. No, our best bet is to stay right here and try to do something about that rock slide in front of the entrance. Do you have a match?"

"No, Max."

"Well, I guess I'll have to use my lighter, then," Max said.

A moment later, a small flame appeared in the darkness.

Max handed the lighter to 99. "Hold this," he said. "I think I have some escape gadgets in my pockets. I picked up a handful the other day when I was in Research & Development. It's a rare occasion when an escape gadget won't come in handy. I'm always getting locked in closets and bath— Ah! Here's something," he said, extracting a pellet-like device from his trousers pocket. He read the instructions on the tag attached to the device. " 'Crush pellet in keyhole. Stand back. Stick fingers in ears.' Well, that doesn't seem too difficult," he said. "Evidently the powder you get when you crush the pellet explodes, blowing the door right off its . . . Mmmmmm . . . we don't seem to have a door, do we? No matter how you look at it, there's just no keyhole in that rock slide." He dropped the pellet to the floor of the tunnel. "Absolutely useless."

"Max—"

"Don't say it, 99! I know—not only is it littering to drop a pellet on a tunnel floor, but it's also—in this case—dangerous. Somebody could come along and step on it and crush it and—and POW! But, don't worry. I'll make sure that doesn't happen. I'll get rid of it." He put his foot on the pellet and crushed it. "Now, there's no danger that somebody will come along and step on it and— Oh-oh!"

"Max!"

Max and 99 raced deeper into the tunnel. They stopped. They stuck their fingers in their ears. A second later there was a tremendous explosion. When the dust cleared, they walked back to the entrance to the tunnel. The rock slide was still in place. Now, however, there was a gigantic hole in front of the entrance.

"Max . . . if you'd crushed that pellet on the rock slide—"

"Don't be a Monday morning quarterback, 99," Max said. "Nobody likes a secret agent and wife who's a Monday morning quarterback." He dug into his pocket again. "Instead of casting the first stone, let's light a little candle in the darkness and see what else we have," he said. "Well . . . what have we here . . ." He held up a device that looked like a skeleton key. "I don't believe it!" he said. "R&D must still be living in the Dark Ages. Imagine. In this day of laser beams and space travel and organ transplants, they still classify an old-time skeleton key as an escape device. Not only is it ridiculous, it's useless, too." He tossed the device into the darkness.

"Max," 99 began, "don't you think—"

There was a glow of light from the direction in which Max had thrown the key.

"That glow looks very familiar," Max said.

"I think you really should have read the instructions on the key, first, Max," 99 said.

"Who needs instructions to operate a skeleton key?"

"Maybe it wasn't—"

"I know!" Max said. "That's the glow of a laser beam. 99, that key isn't a key, it's a laser beam! Good old R&D! They disguised—"

The glow faded.

Carrying the lighter, Max made his way through the darkness to where the key had landed. He picked it up and read the instructions that were still attached to it. Then he tossed the key away again.

"Yes, Max . . . what?" 99 said.

"Good old R&D booted it again," Max informed her. "They designed a laser to look like a skeleton key. Nobody would read the instructions to a skeleton key to find out that it was a laser."

"But can't it still be used, Max?"

"The battery is dead," Max replied. "That's another goof. They should have designed it as a wind-up laser." He started going through his pockets again. "Well, if at first you don't succeed, try, try—"

Max was interrupted by a sudden blinding flash. Automaticaly, he and 99 threw up their arms to protect their eyes. A moment later, when they looked, they were startled to find that they were no longer alone. Standing before them was a grizzled old man with a heavy beard. He was wearing rough clothes and boots and holding a lantern. And beside him was a scraggly-looking mule, that had a pack and a pick and shovel strapped to its back.

"Howdy," the old man said. "If you're lost and looking for the way back, it's right through that pile of rocks."

Max and 99 looked at the rocks that were still piled in the entrance.

"How did you get in here?" Max asked.

"I materialized—that's the technical term," the old man replied. "If you want *my* opinion, though, it's magic." He frowned. "I guess you don't recognize who I am," he said. "I'm the resident ghost in this here ghost town. You can't have a ghost town without you have a ghost, can you? Years and years ago, I was a prospector in these hyar hills. But I got caught in this tunnel and sealed in by a rock slide—just like that rock slide that's blocking the door right now. Well . . . it turned out to be fatal. So, now I'm a ghost."

"That's a lit-tle bit hard to believe," Max said. "How about that mule? Don't tell me the mule is a ghost, too."

"The mule's a ghost, too," the old prospector said.

"I believe I asked you not to tell me that. But, now that you have, you might as well know that I refuse to believe it. I can accept the idea of a ghost prospector. But a ghost mule?"

The old prospector raised the lantern. "If you can believe in a ghost lantern, you ought to be able to believe in a ghost mule," he said.

"He's got a point there," Max said to 99. He faced back to the prospector. "All right, for the time being, I'll accept the possibility of a ghost prospector, ghost mule and ghost lantern. But what are you doing here in this tunnel? If you had a fatal accident here, I'd think you'd want to get out. That shouldn't be any trouble for a ghost."

"This is the tunnel to the mine," the old prospector explained. "My mule and me, we're doomed to haunt this town and this mine until we find the lost vein of gold."

"Oh, really? Why is that?" Max asked, interested.

"Don't ask me," the old prospector shrugged. "I don't make up the rules. All I know is, I had that fatal accident here in the tunnel a long, long time ago, and when I got up to the pearly gates there was this fella there, and he said to me, 'Where's the gold?' Well, I told him I was still looking for it when I suddenly took sick with that fatal accident. So, he says to me, 'Go back and get the gold, you butterhead. And don't come knocking around the gates 'til you find it.' "

Max looked skeptical. "Is that *all* he said?"

"No. He said to get rid of the mule before I came back, too."

"Oh . . . that's too bad," 99 said sympathetically.

"Yeah, it kind of set my teeth on edge, too," the old prospector said. "On account of that, I just might make a full career out of looking for that lost vein of gold. I'll tell you the truth—I got a look through the gates while I was standing there jawing with that fella. And what I saw was, I saw all these folks sitting around on clouds in a bunch of sheets. They had wings on their backs and they were playing harps. Now, I could take about ten minutes of that. But if I had to put up with it for a whole eternity, I'd be climbing the walls trying to get out. See what I mean?"

"I'll admit to seeing what you mean, but only if it's understood that I don't believe any of this," Max said.

"Deal!" the old prospector grinned, holding out a hand.

Max tried to shake it—but found himself grasping thin air. "Let's make that a verbal agreement," he said. "Now, what can you do about getting us out of here?"

The old prospector looked at him speculatively. "Why would I *want* to get you out of here?" he asked. "I don't know you, young fella. For all I know, you might turn out to be the worst enemy I ever had. I admit, you look kind of dumb. But maybe that's an act."

"It is *not* an act," Max said.

"You're really as dumb as you look, eh? It's hard to believe."

"That's not what I meant," Max said. "What I meant is, I'm not putting on an act of any kind. I'm really exactly what I seem to be—an innocent secret agent in trouble. Maybe it would help if I introduced myself. My name is Smart—"

"Your middle name is smart, you mean?"

"No—my last name. I'm with—"

"Then what's your middle name? Dumb—like it looks?"

"Let's forget the name," Max said. "Just refer to me by my number. I'm 86." He indicated 99. "And this is my wife, 99. You see, we're secret agents. And, instead of being called by name, we're called by number. Understand?"

"All but a couple things," the old prospector replied. "What's a secret agent? And how come you got a number instead of a name?"

"Yes . . . well . . . A secret agent is—in a way— like a private detective—understand?"

"Sure—like a Pinkerton. Now, why do you have numbers in the place of names?"

"That, I'm afraid, I can't answer," Max replied.

"Oh. Too big a secret, eh?"

"Actually, the reason I can't explain it is because I haven't the faintest idea why," Max replied. "All I can tell you is, I don't make the rules."

"That's enough," the old prospector said. "I can understand that." He looked Max and 99 up and down. "Well, I guess you look okay to me," he said, finally.

"Thank you," Max smiled.

"Not you. I was talking about her," the prospector said, winking at 99. "You," he said, facing Max again, "don't look quite right to me. But, if she'll vouch for you—"

"I will," 99 assured the old prospector. "He's really very nice. And honest and trustworthy, too."

"What puzzles me," Max said to the old man, "is why you're so suspicious. You're a ghost—what harm could any of us do you? It seems to me that you're as bad off as you'll ever get."

"You're wrong," the old prospector said. "Suppose somebody else found that lost vein of gold? And mined it? If that happened, it wouldn't be there for me to look for any more. I'd go loopy just wandering around here in this ghost town with nothing to occupy my talents. If it came to that, I'd be just as well off up there behind them gates with them fellas in the sheets and wings. Only, I couldn't get in. Without that gold, they're not even going to let me within smelling distance of the place."

"Yes, well—"

"So, when I saw you strangers pull into town, I disappeared myself," the old prospector said. "I had to find out if you were after my gold or not. Now that I know you're not—according to you—I can disappear myself again and go on about my business. And, you can do the same." He tipped his hat to 99. "So long, ma'am, it's been—"

"Hold it a minute," Max said. "You can't leave us. It's true, we're not after your gold. But I can't promise the same about those other fellows. If they happened to run across your vein of gold, they'd pack it up and ship it out of here quicker than you could bat an eyelash."

"Oh?" the old prospector said. "How come? Aren't they friends of yours?"

"Hardly. They're our worst enemies," Max replied. "We're Control and they're KAOS."

"Like cops and robbers?" the old prospector asked.

"Not exactly," Max responded. "It's just not that simple. Nothing is quite that simple any more. You see, we're all secret agents, both Control and KAOS, but the KAOS secret agents are dedicated to the propagation of evil, while the Control secret agents are dedicated to stamping it out. Although, of course, it's not always that simple. I mean, every once in a while, we're forced to fight fire with fire. Or, in other words, sometimes we have to propagate a little evil ourselves in the interests of stamping out the evil that the KAOS secret agents have propagated earlier—if you understand what I mean. Not that I'd blame you if you didn't. Because nothing is really that simple any more. I mean, looked at from one standpoint, it could be said that in propagating evil to stamp out evil we are tarring ourselves with our own brush, or that we're trying to put out the fire by dousing it with kerosene, or—"

"Can you just tell me how I can tell the good guys from the bad guys?" the old prospector broke in. "If I just know who I'm for and who I'm against, I don't need all that fiddle-faddle."

"Well, I'm afraid it's just not quite that simple," Max answered. "There was a time when you could distinguish the good guys from the bad guys by looking at their hats. The bad guys had on black hats and the good guys had on white hats. But things have changed. A lot of people these days don't wear hats of any color. And, too, bad guys put on white hats, and good guys put on black hats. So, telling a good guy from a bad guy, or, even if you know the difference, really deciding what is essentially good and what is essentially bad is almost— Frankly, it's so complicated, it's absolutely impossible to explain. But, I'll tell you what I do. I have a rule of thumb. I think of it as being like cops and robbers."

"I don't see what's so complicated about that," the old man said. "Who're you—cops or robbers?"

"Actually, it's not as simple—"

"Cops!" 99 shouted.

The old prospector nodded. "Got it. Now," he asked, "what do I do to get them strangers out of here?"

"They're not in here," Max said. "We're the ones who are in here."

"Out of town, I mean!" the old prospector said.

"Oh. Well, actually, that's my job, not yours," Max said. "You could go wave your arms at them or something, but I doubt that it would get rid of them. Not many people believe in ghosts these days. They'd probably only laugh at you. And then they'd disinfect you."

"But I got to get them out," the old prospector said.

"I couldn't agree with you more," Max said. "And 99 and I will be happy to do the job for you. Not only will we remove them from your town, but we will lock them up where they will never get out—so you won't have to worry about them coming back later to look for your lost vein."

" 'Lost vein of gold' say," the prospector requested. "When you call it 'my lost vein' it sounds kind of personal. Too personal to say in front of a lady."

"All right—your lost vein of gold."

"Well, don't think I'm not obliged," the old prospector said. "That's right nice of you. I'll just disappear now and let you get about it. When you finish up, whistle or something, and I'll reappear—if I can—and see you off on your trip to wherever it is you'll be going. In the meantime—"

"Hold it," Max said. "First, there are a couple things you'll have to do for us."

The old prospector nodded knowingly. "Always a catch to it," he said. "Things haven't changed so much. What do you want me to do—split my gold with you?"

Max shook his head. "Nothing like that. First, I want you to get us out of here."

"That might be fixed," the old prospector said.

"Then, help us find our Coolidge-head penny."

The old prospector eyed Max narrowly. "Penny, I know," he said. "Head, I know, too. But what's a Coolidge?"

"That's an ex-president. His head is on the coin. He's wearing an Indian headdress. Feathers."

"Feathers to you, too, bub."

"I mean Coolidge is wearing feathers on his head. But, just so you'll be able to recognize it, it also looks a little like Abraham Lincoln standing on his head. If you have a vivid imagination, that is. The feathers look like his beard."

"But suppose when I find it I look at it upside-down?" the old prospector said. "Then it won't look like Lincoln standing on his head. It'll look like some total stranger right-side-up only with his beard on his head instead of on his chin. How'll I know it's not just some ordinary penny like all the others?"

"That's a problem," Max admitted. "Tell you what. When you find a penny you're in doubt about, check with me. I'll recognize it."

"All right, that's agreed," the old prospector said.

"I'll show you how to get out of here, then I'll pitch in and help you locate that feather-head penny, and then you'll wrap them strangers up and haul them out of town and leave me in peace to look for my lost vein of gold."

"Very neatly put," Max replied. "Although, actually, these days, nothing is really quite that simple. For in—"

"Max, just say 'yes!' " 99 begged.

"Yes," Max said to the old prospector. "Now, how do we get out of here?"

Carrying the lamp and followed by the mule and Max and 99, the old prospector moved to the tunnel entrance. He held the lantern high, inspecting the pile of rocks. "Looks like a job for Madame DuBarry," he said.

"Oh? One of your ghost lady friends?"

"That's my mule," the old prospector replied. He faced the mule and addressed it. "See that pile of rocks there in the doorway hole?" he said. "What I want you to do is, I want you to kick them out of the way."

The mule stared at the rocks for a moment. Then it turned around and with its hind hoofs gave the pile of rocks a vicious kick. The rocks flew in all directions, as if blasted out by an explosion.

"That's marvelous!" Max said.

"Yup. Too bad I didn't think of it a hundred-year-or-so ago when I got caught in this tunnel by a rock slide," the old prospector said. "The idea just come to me a couple days ago. But . . . live and learn, they say, eh?"

Max and 99 hurried from the tunnel. A second later, the old prospector and the mule followed them out into the light. Max pointed toward the cluster of buildings. "They're down there somewhere," he said. "In the hotel, probably. Or perhaps in the barbershop. Or maybe— But, that's not important. First, we'll go to the saloon."

"I'll drink to that," the old prospector said.

"We'll go to the saloon to find the Coolidge-head penny," Max explained. "It dropped through a crack in the floor."

"I got a better idea," the old prospector said. "First, let's lock up them strangers and make lost veins of gold safe for cranky old prospectors, like you said you were going to do. After that, we'll look for the penny."

Max shook his head. "I need the penny first," he said. "You see, I'll rub it. And then the Chief, back in Washington, will get the signal, and he'll send a squad of Control agents out here, and they'll surround the hotel or the barbershop or wherever the KAOS agents are holding their meeting, and they'll take them captive and transport them back to Washington and lock them up. But first I have to— Why are you looking at me that way?"

"You're going to rub a penny and somebody's going to hear it in Washington? I know Indians've got good hearing. But it's not that good."

"What Indians?"

"The Chief, you said."

"The Chief of Control—not an Indian chief," Max explained. "And it's not that he'll hear me rubbing the coin. It isn't as simple as that. This is an electronic— No, that won't mean anything to you, will it? I'll just have to start at the beginning. Once upon a time, you see, there was a Founding Father named Benjamin Franklin who liked to fly his kite in thunder storms. Well, one day—"

"Max," 99 broke in, "couldn't you, just for once, give a simple answer? We don't have time for a full explanation."

"You're right, 99," Max said. He turned back to the old prospector. "It's magic," he said.

"Now, you're making sense," the old man told him.

5.

CAUTIOUSLY, AND AS QUIETLY as possible considering that the pots and pans dangling from the pack on the mule's back were clanging, Max, 99, the old prospector and the mule made their way down the hillside toward the town.

"Can you do something with those pans?" Max said to the old prospector.

"Sure. I cook in them. What do you *think* I have them for? Just to keep the mule from getting lost?"

"What I mean is, isn't there some way you can keep them quiet?"

"Well . . . I don't need them any more, since I don't cook," the old prospector replied. "So, I guess I could get rid of them. A ghost don't eat, you know. Anything a ghost eats, it goes straight on through and drops to the ground. Who wants to eat stuff that's dropping on the ground all the time?"

Max halted the march. "The pans . . . please?"

The old prospector unfastened the pots and pans from the pack and tossed them aside. They went banging and clattering down the hill.

"Why don't you just go down there to the hotel and make a general announcement to those KAOS assassins that we're coming," Max said sarcastically.

"You sure don't know much about sneaking up on folks," the old prospector said. "That's no way to do it. You got to take them by surprise."

Max decided there was nothing to be gained by further discussion. He motioned and proceeded and 99 and the old prospector and the mule tagged after him again. Soon, they reached the bottom of the hill. Then, Max led them into town. When he saw that they would have to pass the hotel, where he assumed the seminar was in progress, to get to the saloon, he signalled the march to a halt.

"We'll have to keep down," he said in a hushed tone. "If those KAOS assassins spot us, all is lost. There are too many of them for us to handle alone. Now, everyone down. Flat on the ground. From here to the saloon, we'll crawl on our bellies."

"That sounds kind of dumb to me," the old prospector said.

"It just so happens that it's a generally accepted military tactic," Max replied. "Haven't you ever heard the phrase 'an army travels on its stomach?' "

"I heard it. But I never believed it," the old prospector said. "How about the mules? Look at Madame DuBarry—you think you're going to get her down on her belly? She's got too much dignity for that."

"All right—everybody stoop, then," Max said, compromising.

The old prospector addressed the mule. "Think you can do that, Madame?" he asked. "Think you can look stoopid like this fella here?"

"Isn't there another way you could phrase that?" Max asked.

"Max—we're wasting so much time!" 99 protested.

"You're right, 99." He turned to the old prospector

again. "The important thing is to get to the saloon," he said. "If you and your mule want to walk upright, that's your business. But 99 and I happen to be experienced secret agents and we know how to do these things, so we'll crawl on our stomachs. Now—ready?"

"Max . . . if it's all the same to you, I think I'll walk upright, too," 99 said. "This dress just came back from the cleaners, and I don't see—"

"Well, *I'll* crawl!" Max said disgustedly. And he dropped to the ground and began slithering through the dust toward the saloon.

99 and the old prospector and the mule ambled along behind.

"He does that good," the old prospector remarked to 99.

"He's had a lot of practice," she replied. "He drops his cuff links a lot, and they always roll under the bed, and he always has to crawl under after them."

"He's sure got to be expert," the old prospector said, genuinely impressed. "If there was any demand for that kind of thing, I bet he could make a good living at it." He addressed the mule. "Watch that technique," he said. "You might want to crawl under a fence someday, and that's the way to do it. You might have a little trouble pulling yourself forward with your elbows, though. I never noticed that before—you got no elbows, Madame."

The mule hee-hawed.

"True, true," the old prospector nodded.

Max stopped crawling and got to his feet. "What did she say?" he asked the old prospector, indicating the mule.

"He's not a she, he's a he," the old prospector replied.

"A he? Named Madame DuBarry?"

"That was his idea, not mine," the old prospector said. "I didn't give him a name at all when I got him. I figured that ought to be his right, picking a name for himself. So, for the first nine years I just called him 'Hey, you!' Then, on his tenth birthday, I told him to take any name he wanted. Madame DuBarry was the pick. He figured being French it had class."

"I'll accept that," Max said. "Now, what was it he replied when you made that comment about him not having any elbows?"

"He said it saves him the trouble of sewing patches on his sweaters."

Remaining upright, Max moved on toward the saloon once more. The others hurried after him. As Max neared the entrance to the saloon, however, he abruptly halted. He cocked his head, listening. Then he gestured urgently to the others, signalling them to flatten themselves against the side of the building.

"What is it?" 99 whispered.

"Somebody's in there!" Max whispered back. "I heard a voice—talking. Let's get close to a window. Maybe we can hear what's going on."

Quietly and warily, they advanced to a window. They could all hear the voice, then.

"It's Arbuthnot!" 99 said. "What's he doing—talking to himself?"

"I don't think so, unfortunately," Max replied. "Evidently the seminar is being held in the saloon instead of in the hotel. All those assassins must be in there."

"I see—it's the KAOS assassins he's addressing," 99 nodded. "Then, that means—"

"It means we can't get in there to look for the Coolidge-head penny," Max said gloomily. "Unless— Let's listen. The meeting may break up soon. Then, when the KAOS assassins leave, we can slip in and find the penny."

"We might pick up some helpful hints, too, listening," 99 said. "After all, Arbuthnot is recognized as the master. Even around Control he's known as the assassins' assassin."

"Shhhhh!" Max said. He stood on tippytoes to get closer to the window in order to be able to hear better.

"The important thing, when you get an assignment to assassinate some sick person, is not to get that sick person's germs," Arbuthnot was saying. "Or, in the words of the prohet: 'What does it profit an assassin to carry out his mission and then come down with pneumonia?' "

"That makes a lot of sense," Max said to 99.

"Shhhh—I don't want to miss any of this!"

"There is a lot of agitation these days for a code of ethics for assassins," Arbuthnot went on. "And, regarding that, I would like to say that, in my personal opinion, what is needed is not a code of ethics for assassins, but a code of ethics for assassins' victims!"

There were cheers.

"And, thinking along that line," Arbuthnot continued, "I have compiled a list of rules that I think victims ought to be compelled to abide by. Let's see what you think of the list. Now, number one, all victims ought to be completely disinefected at least one hour prior to the assassination. Free disinfection clinics ought to be set up for those victims for whom the process would cause economic hardship. I, personally, do not want to assassinate anybody knowing that he, she or it will end up in debt because of it. Agreed?"

Again, cheers.

"Number two," Arbuthnot resumed, "all victims should be penalized for not covering their mouths when coughing during an assassination. There are enough diseases going around as it is. Let's not start any epidemics."

"Hear! Hear!" the assassins cried.

"And, three," Arbuthnot went on, "no assassin will be required to sneak up barefoot on any victim who has athlete's foot. I consider this the most important rule of all. It is not generally known, but I still have an itch I picked up in '46. You might say that I am my victim's victim."

"That's sheer poetry," Max said to 99, the old prospector and the mule. "But we better not stay here and listen any more. This meeting could go on for hours yet. And the longer we stay here, the greater the chance is that we'll be spotted." He motioned to them and then led them a short distance away. "We better hide somewhere until night," he said. "Then, after dark, we can come back and look for the Coolidge-head penny. Any suggestions on where we could hide?"

"Me and Madame DuBarry can just disappear," the old prospector said.

"For the time being, let's stick together," Max said. "Seeing is believing, you know. If I couldn't see you, I'd probably stop believing in ghosts. And that would be unfortunate because we need every pair of eyes we can muster to look for that Coolidge-head penny."

"We better not stay in town, Max," 99 said. "Before long, the assassins will probably find out that we're not still in that abandoned mine. And they'll start looking for us. They'll begin, I imagine, by searching all the buildings in town."

"You're right," Max replied. "We'll have to get out of the city." He turned to the old prospector. "Where is the nearest suburb?" he asked.

"Come again?"

"Where is 'yonder'?" Max translated.

"Oh. Well, yonder is up in them mountains."

"Good," Max decided. "We'll hide in the mountains

until after dark." He frowned. "We won't get lost in the mountains, will we?" he asked the prospector.

The old man chuckled. "Me and Madame DuBarry know them mountains like we know the inside of a gnat's ear," he said.

"Not at all—right?"

"That about sums it up," the old prospector nodded. "But, you can't get lost on a mountain. All you got to do is keep going downhill and you're bound to get to the bottom sooner or later."

"I wonder why people who get lost on mountains never think of that?" Max mused.

"They're not deep thinkers," the old prospector said. "Tell you the truth, I never wouldn've thought of it, either. It was Madame DuBarry that give me the idea."

"Animal instinct," Max guessed. He looked toward the peak of the nearest mountain. "We better get started," he said.

Max, 99, the old prospector and the mule left town. They soon reached the foot of the hills, then began the climb up the mountain. The incline was fairly steep and they proceeded slowly. By evening they were approximately halfway to the top. Max decided to stop.

"We'll make camp here," he announced. "One of us will build a fire and the rest of us will fan out and look for game."

"Max, if we build a fire, the assassins will see it and know we're up here."

"That's a good point, 99. No fire. Let's just fan out and look for game. We'll have to eat it raw. It won't be pleasant. But if we keep in mind the fact that the free world is depending on our survival, I think we'll be able to do it."

"The free world can go take a flying jump at a tulip bulb," the old prospector said. "You're not going to get me to eat any raw game! I'd die first!"

"You're already dead," Max pointed out.

"It's the spirit that counts," the old prospector said. "I wouldn't eat no raw game when I was alive, either." He pointed to the pack on the mule's back. "What do you think's in there?" he said. "I always toted my own goodies. Now that I'm a ghost, I don't eat no more. But, if you two are hungry . . ."

Max looked at the pack warily. "Let's see what you have." he said.

The old prospector opened up the pack. "Well . . . let's see . . ." he said, looking inside. "We've got some *les pattes de crabe vinaigrette,* and some *filets de triute vauclusienne,* and some *fonds d'artichauts,* and some *caneton froid à la Montmorency,* and some *carre d'agneau roti.*" He faced back to Max. " 'Course, none of it's fresh—it's all canned," he said apologetically.

Max and 99 stared into the pack, flabbergasted.

"He's right! It's all there!" Max said. He turned to the old prospector. "That's fantastic!" he said. "How do you do it?"

"It's not my doing," the old man replied. "It's Madame DuBarry's."

"Then how does he do it?"

"Well . . . I've give it some thought over the years," the old prospector said, "and I've finally figured out that, with a name like DuBarry, it's on account of he must really be French."

"I guess that's as good an explanation as any," Max nodded. He reached into the pack. "I'll just have some of this *les pattes de crabe vinaigrette* for starters," he said. "How long has he been packing these delicacies around, anyway?"

"Oh, years and years and years and years," the old prospector replied. "Since long before we got caught in that abandoned mine and turned to ghosts."

"You mean you've never had any of it?" Max said.

"Nope."

"That's hard to believe. Why not?"

"No can opener," the old prospector explained.

"Oh."

Max tossed the can of *les pattes de crabe vinaigrette* back into the pack.

"Shall I go look for some game, Max?" 99 said sympathetically.

Max shook his head. "For health reasons, I think I'll go hungry," he replied.

"Raw game wouldn't hurt you, Max."

"It might not do anything to my stomach," he said. "But eating raw squirrel, with all those delicacies around, would probably break my heart." He sat down on a stump. "Let's talk about something besides food," he said.

"I know some tall tales," the old prospector said, squatting. "Tall tales always help to pass the time."

"Better than that, how about some ghost stories," Max suggested.

The old prospector shuddered. "To scary," he said. "Anyway, all my ghost stories have sad endings. All 'cept one—the story about the Indian that died and become a ghost and went to the happy haunting ground. Me, personal, though, I didn't hit it that lucky. If I had it to do all over again, I'd be almost anything but a ghost. Too many drawbacks."

"For instance?"

"Well, when Madame DuBarry and me are disappeared we're always running into and straight through each other. Ever have a mule walk through your chest? It gives you a funny feeling."

"I can imagine," Max replied.

"And you get so you don't pay any attention to whether you're disappeared or appeared," the old prospector said. "I got a habit of tightening my bandana up tight around my neck—sort of like a rube necktie. Well, it's all right when I do it and I'm disappeared. It just tightens up into a hard knot. But when I do it when I'm appeared—thinking I'm disappeared—I sometimes like to strangle myself."

"Yes, well—"

"But the biggest drawback of all—not just for me, but for Madame DuBarry, too—is, we still haven't quite got the hang of disappearing and appearing. Myself, I've got a little quirk where when I raise my right arm I sometimes just disappear right out from under myself. And Madame DuBarry has to watch out how he switches his tail."

"That doesn't seem to be—"

"What's bad about it is," the old prospector went on, "we sometimes disappear for weeks or months and can't reappear again for the life of us. Madame DuBarry was gone the whole month of April back in '52. And me, I missed the winter of '61 altogether. I reached up with my right hand to pick a leaf off a tree in late September and I didn't get back untl long past March."

"Well, I suppose that—"

"Missed Christmas completely. New Year's Day, too. I guess I shouldn't complain, though. I missed my birthday—which is in February—too. So, that makes me a year younger than I really am. Not that it does me any good. Being dead, I can't look forward to living a year longer. Outside every silver lining, there's a dark cloud." He looked up into the sky. "Speaking of that," he said. "It's coming on dark. Maybe we better get started back toward town."

"Good idea," Max said, rising. "By the time we get there, the assassins will probably all be in bed asleep. That will give us a chance to search for the Coolidge-head penny. Ready, 99?" he asked.

"Yes, Max." She peered into the dimness. "I'm just glad we have a guide to lead us back," she said. "I

don't think I could find my way to town again even if
it is all downhill."

"I doubt that I could, either," Max said. He addressed the old prospector. "Which way is it?" he
asked.

"Follow me," the old man replied. And he raised his
right arm and waved—and immediately disappeared.

"I guess that proves it—he *does* have trouble with
his disappearing and appearing," Max said. "Did you
see that, 99? He raised his right arm—and POOF!"
He looked at his watch. "Let's see how long it takes
him to reappear."

"I just hope we don't have to wait until next
March," 99 said worriedly.

"So do I. I'd hate to miss Christmas." He raised his
arm and shook his wrist. "I think my watch has
stopped," he said. "The hands keep going around—"
He put it to his ear. "—and it's still ticking—" He
shrugged, puzzled. "—but the old prospector hasn't
reappeared."

"Max . . . maybe we better try to find our way back
ourselves."

"And get lost, 99? What would that accomplish?"

"We'd be doing something. What are we accom-
plishing now, just standing here?"

"99, we're not *just* standing here. We're standing
here and waiting. There's a difference. The old prospector will be back in a minute or so."

"The last time—"

"I know about the last time. The last time he
missed the whole winter of '61. But this is not the last
time. This is this time." Max looked around nervously.
"You're right—we better start worrying," he said. He
peered into the darkness. "Prospector?" he called.
"Are you out there?" There was no response. Max
looked at the mule. "Maybe we ought to send Madame
DuBarry after him," he said.

"Fine. But how?"

Max faced the mule. *"Parlez-vous Francais?"*

"Max, just because his name is Madame DuBarry, that doesn't mean he speaks French."

"It's just as well," Max said. "We wouldn't be able to converse, anyway. I speak French fluently, but, unfortunately, I don't understand a word of it." He addressed the mule again. "I'll try to make this as simple as possible," he said. "Remember the old prospector who was around here a little earlier? Sic 'em!"

The mule stared back at Max.

"Mules are the dumbest of all beasts," Max said to 99. "This one is stupid in two languages, English and French."

"Hee-Haw!" the mule protested.

"He's even poor in mule," Max said. "I didn't understand a word of that!"

Looking annoyed, the mule switched its tail aggitatedly—and disappeared.

"Oh, Max!" 99 said. "Now, we're completely alone."

"Take it easy, 99. Maybe Madame DuBarry went looking for the old prospector."

"Do you believe that, Max?"

He shook his head. "It's my honest opinion, 99, that we just lost the mule, too. I guess we'll have to try to make it back to town without a guide." He looked around. "Which way is down?"

"That way, I think—" 99 said, pointing. "I think I remember seeing a path over in that direction."

"That's not enough, 99. Was it a path going up or a path going down?"

"Let's try it and find out," 99 suggested. "If it goes up, we can turn around and take it in the other direction. It won't go up in both directions?"

"How can we be so sure about that?" Max asked.

"99—be honest with me, now—have you been up on this mountain before?"

"Max, of course not!"

"I hope not. When we told each other everything about our pasts before we got married, you didn't say a word about being up here on this mountain and knowing so much about the paths."

"Max . . honest! It was only a wild guess when I said the path couldn't go up on both ends."

"All right." Max got 99 by the hand and moved cautiously into the darkness. "We'll go slowly," he said. "It seems to be headed downward, just as you said, 99. I hope it's just coincidence. If I ever find out that—Oops!"

"Who bumped me?" a voice asked.

"Old prospector?" Max asked. "Is that you?"

"It's either me or my mule," the voice replied. "We been together so long, sometimes I have trouble telling us apart. You that secret agent, Max 86?"

"Yes and no," Max replied. "The name is Max Smart. It's the number that's 86. Where have you been, anyway?"

"Trying to get back," the voice replied. "But I'm here, now. Let's not waste a lot of time jawing. Follow me and I'll lead you down."

"Where are you?" Max asked.

"Over here."

"Oh . . . yes . . . I can see you now . . . very dimly. All right, we're ready."

"Follow me," the voice said, "this way. We'll be—"

"Max! What happened?" 99 asked.

"I'm not sure," Max replied. "He raised his right arm and waved and that was the last I saw of him."

6.

DEPRIVED OF THE EXPERT ASSISTANCE of the old prospector, Max and 99 started down the mountain path alone again in the darkness.

"Max . . . I can't see a thing!" 99 complained.

"I can't either, 99. I wonder why we can't see the town. Surely, those assassins must have at least one lantern lit."

"Maybe they didn't bring kerosene."

"A candle, then."

"Assassins just aren't known for lighting candles in the darkness, Max."

"I guess you're right. But— 99 . . . are you whispering?"

"No, Max. But I was just going to ask you the same thing. I can hardly hear you."

"Uhhhh . . . 99, do you have the feeling you're going uphill again? I do. And if you don't, that probably means that we're no longer together. Or, to put it another way, that somehow we separated, and you're still going down, while I'm going up."

"I think we separated, Max. Turn around and come

back this way. I'll keep talking so you can follow the
sound of my voice. How am I coming in? Can you
hear me better now?"

"Perfectly, 99."

"Oh! You startled me. Where are you, right next to
me?"

"I'm ahead of you again, 99. Let's go. Follow me."

"Max . . . maybe we better hold hands."

"99, we did that all through the courting. Now that
we're married, can't we cut out all that goopy stuff?
We'll have to sooner or later, anyway, when we have
children. You know how kids hate that goopy stuff.
You wouldn't want to lose the respect of the children,
would you, 99? They might switch to another chan-
nel."

"They might do *what*, Max?" 99 asked, baffled.

"Uhh . . . run away from home, I meant. The new
generation is very TV-conscious, I understand. So, naturally, some of the television terminology gets into the
everyday language. I practice bridging the generation
gap every chance I get—terminology-wise, that is—in
case we have children of our own some day."

"Do you want children, Max?"

"Of course, 99."

"Then I think we better continue holding hands
every once in a while. That's how it begins."

"No kidding!" Max said. "My mother always told
me she got me at the grocery store."

"Max, have you ever seen any children on sale at
the A&P?"

"Of course not, 99. But I was born in the days of
the corner grocery, when you could get personal service. So, I just naturally figured that— 99, have you
noticed that we're not going downhill again any
more?"

"Yes, Max. But we're not going uphill, either. I
think we must be down from the mountain. Now all

we have to do is find our way back to the town again. It ought to be— Oh, sorry, Max."

"My fault—I should have warned you I intended to stop. I want to try to get my bearings. As I recall, the mountain was back that way. So, logically, the town ought to be over that way. Is that how you remember it, 99?"

"Max, I can't see where you're pointing."

"Oh . . . yes . . . well, let me put it another way. that puts the town to my right. Do you— Uhhhhh, you can't see me, so you don't know my right from my left —right?"

"Right, Max." 99 replied. "But, may I make a suggestion?"

"Go right ahead."

"Max, if you think the town is to the right, then— considering the various experiences we've had in the past—I think we better look for it on the left. I mean, you're a great hand-holder, Max, but as a direction-finder, you leave a lot to be desired. I hope you won't resent my frankness."

"Of course not, 99. Two people, when they're married, I think, *should* be frank with each other. Just one word of caution, though, 99. If you have anything frank to say about my breath, I think you better not do it. If you do, our marriage is going to be in big trouble."

"Honest, Max, you have a very nice breath."

"Oh. Well, that's the kind of frankness I can accept. It's the other kind that I find so objectionable. However, we'll look for the town on the left, anyway. Because now, after all this delay, I'm so turned-around, I don't know which was my right and which was my left. And, consequently, by going left we will probably be going right—which will prove that I was right in the first place." He got hold of 99's hand. "Come on."

Again, Max and 99 struck out into the darkness.

"99," Max said, "there's something that puzzles me. Why is it that you were never as frank with me while we were courting as you've been since we got married?"

"Well, Max, you might not have been interested in marrying me if you'd realized how frank I can be sometimes. But, now that we're married, what can you do about it? I mean, you can't get a divorce on the grounds that I'm frank. Frankness is a very admirable trait. The court would just tell you that you ought to be happy to have a wife who was so frank."

"The court hasn't ever had its direction-findingness sneered at," Max grumbled. "That wasn't very nice of you, 99. When did you ever hear of any other wife complaining about her husband's direction-findingness?"

"Most wives don't have any cause to complain about that, Max," 99 replied. "After they're married, they don't have to worry about finding directions because their husbands never take them anywhere."

"Oh. Well, you can't say that about our marriage," Max commented. "Remember last month when I took you to that mass poisoning planned by KAOS for the meeting of the International Brotherhood for Non-Violent Peace Negotiations Association delegates? And the week after that when I took you to that trap that KAOS had planned for us and we nearly lost our heads in that pair of matching guillotines? And now, here we are again, out on the town, wandering around in the dark, surrounded by KAOS assassins."

"You're right, Max," 99 admitted. "We have something most married couples don't have. Not once since we've been married have I had cause to complain that you don't take me anywhere. But, frankly, Max—"

"Forget it, 99. If you want to continue to be invited along to mass poisonings, you'll lay off that frankness."

"All right, Max. Max . . . isn't it getting a little lighter?"

"I noticed that, too, 99. It's my guess that one of those KAOS assassins decided to turn over a new leaf. He's probably celebrating by lighting a candle in the darkness."

"Either that, Max, or dawn is breaking."

"Yes . . . I suppose it could be that," Max said. "As a matter of fact, isn't that the sun over there? That orange glow on the horizon, I mean."

"Yes! And I can see you again, Max!"

"And I can see you, too, 99. And I can also see— 99, look where we are."

99 looked around. She and Max were standing in the middle of a dusty street, smack-dab in the center of town. "Oh, Max!" she said disgustedly. "There's the saloon over there. We're only about fifty yards from it. All this time we've been wandering around in the darkness, we could have been searching for the Coolidge-head penny in the saloon! We've wasted so much time!"

"Let's just not waste any more," Max said. And he headed hurriedly toward the saloon, which was on the other side of the hotel.

As Max and 99 were passing the entrance to the hotel, however, Arbuthnot suddenly appeared from the doorway. He was dressed in a gray sweatsuit and was trotting. The instant he spotted Max and 99 he drew a pistol from inside his sweatshirt, where, apparently, he had a shoulder holster, pointed it at them and ordered them to halt.

"And face the other direction—you're breathing your germs on me!" Arbuthnot said irritably. "What's the world coming to, anyway! A man gets up at the crack of dawn and goes out for a little jogging, and what does he meet right outside his door? Germ-spreaders!"

"Anybody who can jog at the crack of dawn deserves anything terrible that happens to him," Max answered. "Nice people can't even crawl to the breakfast table at the crack of dawn, let alone make it to the street to go jogging."

"Turn around!" Arbuthnot snapped.

"Aren't you worried about our germs?"

"That's why I want you to turn around. I just tested, and the breeze is blowing from that direction. I want you to turn around and change places with me. That will put you downwind. Come on—snap it up!"

Max and 99 and Arbuthnot changed places. Arbuthnot moved to the street, and Max and 99 took his place on the porch of the hotel.

"Now, we'll jog," Arbuthnot informed them. He pointed. "We'll go that way with the wind. You lead and I'll follow. Not too fast, though. Too fast is running, not jogging. Ready?"

"Just a minute," Max objected. "I think, according to the rules, you're allowed to lock us up again or assassinate us. But jogging is out. That's an indignity that I insist on being spared. Suppose somebody I know saw me jogging around town at the crack of dawn? It's all right with me if *you* want to be known as a nut, Arbuthnot, but I refuse to let you force me to get myself into the same situation. The answer is no. An unqualified no."

Arbuthnot shrugged. "Well, I always jog at this time in the morning," he said, "and I have no intention of disrupting my routine. So," he said, raising his pistol, "I guess I'll just have to assassinate you."

"I'll jog," Max decided.

"That-a-way!" Arbuthnot said, pointing downwind.

Max and 99 jogged down the steps from the porch, then jogged up the street, with Arbuthnot a few steps behind them.

"Right at the bank," Arbuthnot ordered. "Then left

THE GHASTLY GHOST AFFAIR

at the jail, right again at the bakery, another right at the blacksmith's shop, left at the cafe, left, right, left at the watering trough, general store and saloon, then right again at the stable. Got that?"

"I don't think so," Max replied, continuing to jog. "Maybe you better come up here and lead and we'll go back there and hold the gun."

"Don't get smart, Smart!"

Max and 99 turned right at the bank, then a few minutes later, took a left at the jail.

Keeping his voice low, Max said, "I think I know how to get out of this, 99. If we play it right, we can lose Arbuthnot. Remember the instructions he gave us? Well, where he told us to jog, instead, we'll jag."

"I don't think I quite understand that, Max."

"When we get to the bakery, where he told us to turn right, we'll turn left, instead," Max explained. "Then left at the blacksmith's shop, and right at the cafe, right, left, right at the watering trough, general store and saloon, then—"

"Max," 99 broke in, "when we get to the saloon, rather than turning right, why don't we go in?"

"That would disrupt the routine, 99. If jogging is going to do you any good at all, you have to establish a regimen for yourself and stick to it. Consistency is the secret to—"

"Max! It's Arbuthnot who's interested in jogging, not us. We're interested in the Coolidge-head penny. And the penny is in the saloon."

"All right, then," Max said, "instead of a left at the blacksmith's shop, we'll take— Better yet, 99, just follow me. When we reach the bakery, I'm going to take a left. After that, I'll play it by ear, always keeping firmly in mind, of course, that our ultimate destination should be the saloon."

"I'll be right behind you, Max."

A few seconds later, they reached the bakery. Max

cut sharply to the left, and 99 stayed right behind him.

"Stop!" they heard Arbuthnot shout angrily. "You're disrupting the routine!"

"This way!" Max called, racing around a corner. "Are you still with me, 99?"

"I'm here, Max!"

"Now, through the blacksmith shop!" Max said. "Then around the watering trough, past the general store, through the jail, and into the saloon!"

"I'm right with you, Max!"

Running as fast as he could move, Max led the way around the blacksmith shop, then through the watering trough—which, fortunately, was dry—then around the general store, then into the jail and into a cell.

"Max, that window has bars on it," 99 pointed out.

"You're right, 99. Back the other way."

They whipped around and ran in the other direction. But not far. Two feet later they crashed into the closed and locked cell door. On the other side, facing them, was Arbuthnot.

"Max! What happened!" 99 wailed.

"Evidently we took a left when we should have taken a right," Max replied. "It could happen to anybody, 99. I've never jogged in this town before." He looked puzzledly at Arbuthnot. "But how did you know you'd find us here?" he asked.

"It had to happen," Arbuthnot replied. "When I saw you jogging through the watering trough, I said to myself, 'Anybody with a brain like that, he's going to trap himself in a cell over in the jail house.' So, I just trotted over here, and here you were."

"You have a very frank way of putting things," Max told him. "You'd make somebody a terrible wife."

"I'm sorry I can't stay," Arbuthnot said, leaving. "But old jails are usually crawling with germs." He went out the doorway, then closed the door behind him.

"Locked in with all these germs," Max muttered.

99 went back to the window. "I can see the hotel from here, Max," she reported. "There's Arbuthnot. He's going inside."

"99 . . ."

She turned toward him. "Yes, Max?"

Max pointed to the cot, the only item of furniture in the cell. "It just moved," he said.

"Max . . . you're imagining . . ."

"I tell you, it just— See that! It did it again!"

"Yes! I saw it, too!" 99 said, staring wide-eyed at the cot. "Max, do you think the cell is haunt—" She suddenly brightened. "Max, of course! It's probably the old prospector! We can't see him because he's disappeared! But he's here! He's here with us!"

"A lot of good that does," Max said.

"I guess you're right," 99 agreed gloomily. She went back to the window. "Look, Max," she said. "One of the KAOS assassins just came out of the hotel and he's carrying a tray of food and heading this way."

Max joined her at the window. "Arbuthnot probably sent him to feed us," he said. "We wouldn't be very valuable as hostages if we starved to death. Listen, 99, when that assassin gets here, let's try to lure him into the cell. Then we can overpower him and escape."

"We can try," 99 said. "He probably won't even speak to us, though."

"99, don't judge all KAOS assassins by Arbuthnot," Max said reprovingly. "That's not fair. Frankly, in general, I've found most KAOS assassins to be genial, friendly, polite and genuinely interested in other people's welfare—assuming, of course, that those other people aren't marked for assassination."

"Maybe so, Max, but—"

At that moment, the jail door opened, and the KAOS assassin, a young, blond, smiling young man, entered, carrying a tray of food. "Hi y'all," he grinned, moving to the cell door. "The boss man told me to tote you over some victuals. He figures you must have a powerful hunger by now." He frowned, looking into the cell. "Why, that's a terrible place in there," he said. "You got no carpet on the floor, the whole shebang needs a new coat of paint, that window hasn't got nary a curtain on it, and that—" He shook his head in sorrow. "It's too terrible even to talk about. Say, how'd you like to have some new furnishings? Maybe a couple nice comfy overstuffed chairs and some nice reading lamps and—" He got a key from his pocket. "Hold it a minute—I'll come in there, and we'll plan on what we can do to redecorate the place."

"See how nice they can be," Max said to 99, as the KAOS assassin opened the door and then entered the cell. "Now, aren't you ashamed of yourself for thinking what you were thinking?"

"I suppose so, Max," 99 nodded. Then she whispered, "Don't forget . . . we're going to over—"

"If you'll just step aside there, ma'am," the assassin said to 99, interrupting her, "I'll put this tray down on that cot, then we can put our minds to what we're going to do to dandy this li'l ol' cell up a bit." He pointed to the area behind Max. "Now, that whole wall has just *got* to come out!" he said. "Why, there's not enough room in here to thread a needle. We'll join that cell next door with this cell, and then we'll build both up and down. I mean, the roof is just crying out for a couple dormers. We can get two bedrooms up there. And a recreation room in the basement, of course." He pointed in another direction. "That window is almost down on its knees, pleading for organdy," he said. "Can't you just *see* it?"

"Now, just a minute!" Max said crisply. "I'll go along with the two bedrooms and the rec room. But you'll put organdy on that window over my dead body!"

The young KAOS assassin drew a pistol. "Now, you're talking my language," he said.

"Organdy on the window."

"Max!" 99 whispered. "Overpower!"

"99 is right," Max said to the KAOS assassin, "organdy would be too overpowering. Even if you doubled the space by knocking out that wall and joining the two cells. But, what we could do—" He motioned to 99. "99, will you step back, please— What we could do," he continued, addressing the young man again, "is knock out this front wall, too, and add what is now the jail house office to the cell. That would give us depth, you see, in addition to width."

The young man was shaking his head. "Guests would walk right into the cell," he said. "You don't want that. Did you see all that dust out there? What do you think it turns to when it rains?" He shuddered. "Mud! A sea of mud! You want that gooey, slimy, dirty old mud tracked in here?"

"You're right," Max said, pained.

"With organdy curtains, though, nobody might notice the mud," the young man said. "That's the choice, as I see it—it's either bare windows with, or organdy windows without, or a combination of the both. You think about it. And when I come back with your lunch, you tell me what you decided."

"Fine, fine, that sounds fair," Max said. "I only hope—"

"Max!" 99 said grimly. "The plan!"

"It's too soon for a plan, 99. We don't know yet whether we want the windows bare or with— Oh! Oh, *that* plan!" He turned back to the young KAOS assassin. "Don't rush off," he said. "Why don't you put down your pistol and rest a while. That's hard work carrying that tray across the street from the hotel. Stay and have breakfast with us."

"Say, that's neighborly of you," the young man

smiled. "I already et once, but I guess another—" He was staring baffledly at the tray. "Where'd the food go?" he asked.

Max and 99 peered at the tray, too. The dishes were now completely empty.

"We must have mice," Max said.

"No mice et all that!" the young man said. He looked around suspiciously. "Who else is in here? You got a stowaway in this cell?"

"Now, does that make sense?" Max replied. "Why would anybody stow away in this cell? It isn't going anyplace."

"Yeah . . . I guess you're right about that," the young assassin said. "Well . . . maybe it *was* a mice that et that food. I don't know . . . I don't like the looks of it, though."

"All right, then, sit down and we'll talk it out and try to find an explanation that suits you," Max said. "Sit right there on the edge of the cot with your back to us and—"

The young man backed toward the cell door. "No, I got to be going," he said. "We're having our seminar meeting over to the bank today, and I don't want to miss any of it. Arbuthnot's going to coach us on combining safe-cracking and assassinating all in one. If you don't know just how, you can get yourself into some bad trouble. We had a fellow in KAOS once who tried it and what he did was, he locked his victim in the safe instead of assassinating him and then he couldn't crack the safe to get in and get at him. He got so frustrated they finally had to send him to a rest farm."

"That's terrible," Max said sympathetically.

"You think that's bad? The victim ended up even worse. He's still locked in the safe. And that was back in the winter of '61."

"That was a big winter for strange occurrences," Max said.

The young man saluted with the pistol. "Well, you think about what you want to do with that window, and I'll be back—"

He did not finish the statement. All of a sudden, he shot straight up into the air. His head cracked against the ceiling of the cell, then he became limp, unconscious. Looking under the young man, Max and 99 saw the cause of his sudden accident. Madame Du-Barry, the mule, had materialized beneath him, thrusting him suddenly upward. The young man, knocked senseless, was now seated on the mule's back.

"What timing!" Max said admiringly. "If you'd been ten seconds later, he'd have got away." He picked up the pistol that had dropped to the floor when the young man had abruptly lost consciousness. "I even forgive you for eating all the food," he said to Madame DuBarry. "Or was that you who ate it? Is your master, the old prospector, around anywhere?"

"Max, you'll never get anything out of that mule," 99 said. "Forget about him. Let's get out of here. Since the KAOS assassins will be at the bank, that will give us time to search the saloon and find the Coolidge-head penny."

"You're right, 99! Let's go!"

"Max . . . what about the young man?"

"He's very nice, 99. He has a lot of personality. But I really don't think he'll help us find that penny. Once a KAOS assassin, always a KAOS assassin. He's on the other side."

"I mean we can't just leave him here like this—sitting on a mule. He'll regain consciousness and get down off the mule and tell Arbuthnot that we've escaped."

"Right!"

Max pulled the young man down off the mule's back and put him on the cot. Then he took the key from him. "Outside," he said to 99 and Madame DuBarry.

When they were all on the other side of the cell door, Max locked it. "Anything else?" he said to 99.

She shook her head. "Perfect, Max."

"Good. Now, up on the mule, 99."

"Up on the mule, Max?"

"Trust me, 99."

"Max, I *do* trust you. But it seems to me that if I can trust you, then you ought to be just as willing to explain to me."

"I can see the fairness of that," Max nodded. "What I have in mind, you see, 99, is the possibility that Arbuthnot will miss this young assassin when he doesn't return. If that happens, he'll probably send somebody to look for him. And the somebody he sends will find out that we've escaped. Well, the first thing he'll do is look for tracks. And he'll find our tracks in the dusty street and he'll know that we're in the saloon. But, if we leave here on the mule, all he'll find is the mule's tracks. He'll never guess that there were two Control agents on top of the mule."

"Max, that's brilliant!"

"Thank you for being so frank, 99. Now . . . up on the mule."

99 got aboard Madame DuBarry. Then Max climbed up and sat behind her.

"Mush!" Max commanded, speaking to the mule.

Madame DuBarry did not move.

"That's for sled dogs, I think, Max," 99 said.

"I know that, 99. What I don't know is the command for mules. So, I used the command that seemed most appropriate. And there's no need, 99, for you to be frank and tell me there's no connection between sled dogs and mules."

"This doesn't seem to be working, Max. He's just standing."

"Giddyap!" Max ordered.

The mule remained immobile.

"I hate to resort to violence," Max said, "but—" He reached back and gave the mule a sound slap on the hindquarters.

Madame DuBarry snorted indignantly, then switched his tail—and disappeared.

Max and 99, deprived of their mount, crashed to the floor.

7.

MAX AND 99 PICKED THEMSELVES from the floor of the jail, where they had landed when Madame DuBarry, the mule, had disappeared.

"The poor thing," 99 said. "The way he comes and goes, I guess he has no control at all over when he appears and disappears."

Max dusted himself off. "If *you* want to believe that, 99, you may," he said. "But it's my guess that that mule knows exactly what it's doing. Why is it that— Whoooooooooops!"

Max was suddenly lifted off his feet and thrust upward. His head cracked against the ceiling. The mule had abruptly reappeared beneath him, and now he was seated precariously astride its neck.

"Max! Are you all right?" 99 cried fearfully.

"Yes . . ." Max replied, rubbing his skull, looking pained. "Don't ask me about the mule, though. I think I would be wise, from now on, to withhold comment on all animals. Unfortunately, I seem to be able to communicate with them."

"Well . . . at least, he's back, Max. Now, we can

90

follow through on your plan to ride him to the saloon. And, you're already on his back—so, in a way, his sudden reappearance was a blessing."

"99, stop looking at the bright side. There are times when looking at the bright side is harder to take than getting batted against the ceiling by a reappearing mule. Now, get up here with me, and— 99, what are you looking at?"

99 had gone to the doorway and opened the door a crack. She was peeping out. "I thought I caught a glimpse of movement out the window," she replied, keeping her voice low. "It was Arbuthnot and the other assassins. They're leaving the hotel!"

"Don't tell me they're coming over here!" Max said.

"No, they're not."

"You're a good wife, 99. I told you not to tell me that, and you didn't. I just wish I could get that kind of cooperation from the KAOS agents. Do you suppose if I married— No, nevermind . . . Where is Arbuthnot going?"

"They seem to be headed . . . Yes, they're going into the bank, Max," 99 reported.

"That fits in with what that assassin who brought our breakfast to us told us," Max said. "The morning meeting is being held in the back. That's perfect! It will give us plenty of time to search the saloon for the Coolidge-head penny. What's happening now, 99?"

"The last one just entered the bank, Max. Now, the door is closing. I think it's safe for us to leave."

"Good. Open the door, 99, so the mule can get out. Then hop up here behind me."

99 opened the door. Immediately, the mule began moving. He strolled through the doorway and across the porch—with 99 alongside, trying to mount.

"Hop up, 99!"

"I can't, Max. He won't stop."

"Then skip!"

"I can't do that, either."

The mule ambled down the porch steps, then out into the street.

"Jump up, 99!"

"Max, I can't hop up, I can't skip up, and I can't jump up. As long as he's moving, there isn't *any* way I can get on him."

"But, 99, you're leaving tracks in the dust!"

"I can't help it, Max!"

The mule, having reached the saloon, strolled up onto the porch, then halted.

Max looked back. "99, why did you tell me you couldn't hop, skip or jump? Look back there! Beside every mule track, there is a hop, skip and jump track."

"Max, I didn't say I couldn't hop, skip or jump. I said I couldn't hop, skip or jump *up*. That 'up' makes a lot of difference."

Max got down from the mule. He looked back at the tracks again. "Well . . . maybe those hop, skip and jump tracks will confuse Arbuthnot," he said. "He probably won't associate them with us. Just looking at us, neither one of us looks like a hopper, skipper and jumper. He'll probably think the mule was accompanied by a drunken jack rabbit."

"We better not stand out here on the porch, Max."

Max nodded agreement, then led the way into the saloon. 99 and the mule followed.

Max pointed to a crack in the floor near the bar. "There!" he said. "That's the crack the Coolidge-head penny dropped through. I'll remember that crack as long as I live."

"Max . . . are you positive that's the crack?" 99 said doubtfully. "I seem to remember that the crack was over here near the tables." She pointed. "Weren't you standing right here by this table, and didn't the penny roll just a few feet and drop down this crack . . . uh, right over here?"

"99, the crack the penny dropped down is etched in my memory. It was that crack right over there."

"That isn't the crack you pointed to first, Max. That crack is almost ten feet from the first crack."

"In the meantime, I changed my mind," Max explained. "I had the actual crack confused with the first crack because the first crack, as you can see, has the same sort of look as the— Well, of course, it doesn't look *exactly* like the actual crack. But the similarity is —" He frowned and peered at the crack that 99 had indicated. "You really think it was this crack over here by the tables, eh?"

"Well, Max . . . now that you mention it . . . I mean, if you're so *positive* that it was one of those cracks over there by the bar, then maybe I'm wrong. After all—"

"99, don't give up so easily," Max said. "Stick to your convictions. If you're absolutely positive that this crack over here is the right crack, then don't let me talk you out of it."

"I'm just not so sure, any more, Max. In fact, now that I recall, I think you're right—it dropped through that crack over there by the bar."

"99, I'm afraid you're wrong. I distinctly remember that the crack was near one of these tables. I said to myself at the time, 'Well, what an attractive-looking table that coin is dropping into a crack near to.' Now, I'm not sure exactly *which* crack by *which* table it was, but the one thing I *do* know is that the crack it dropped into was nowhere near the bar."

99 shrugged. "All right, Max—if you're *that* positive. I agree, it was somewhere over here near the tables."

"Unless, of course, it was near the bar," Max said, scowling again. "It could have rolled farther than I remember. As a matter of fact, now that I remember, it did roll farther than I remember. It probably rolled

allllllll-the-way across the saloon and dropped into one
of those cracks near the bar. Let's start looking there,
anyway."

They walked to the bar, then stood around the crack
that Max had pointed out.

"That looks like it," Max said.

"It looks very crack-like," 99 agreed.

"Hee-haw!" the mule said.

"Is he agreeing or disagreeing, Max?" 99 asked.

"Agreeing, 99."

"Are you sure?"

"That's the nice thing about translating animal talk,
99. You can make it mean anything you want it to
mean." He got down on his knees and put his eye to
the crack. "This is it," he announced.

"Do you see the penny, Max?"

"I see part of it," Max replied, rising. "I see Coolidge's eye."

"His *eye*, Max?"

"What's so surprising about that?" Max asked. "A
Coolidge-head penny has a head, doesn't it? And a
head has an eye—one at the very least—doesn't it?
And the eye in the head of a Coolidge-head penny
would be Coolidge's, wouldn't it? I mean, it would be
a little odd to find Washington's or Lincoln's eye in the
head of a Coolidge-head penny. So, why are you so
surprised that I saw the eye of Coolidge peering up at
me from the head of a Coolidge-head penny?"

"I just sort of thought that if you saw anything,
you'd see the *whole* penny."

"Mmmmmmm . . . come to think of it . . ." He
shrugged. "Well, I saw somebody's eye looking back
up at me," he said. "If it isn't Coolidge's, I think we
better find out whose it is." He looked around the saloon. "I'll need something to use to pry up these floor
boards," he said. "Let's see . . . Aha!" He walked
over to a chair and picked it up, raised it above his

head, then smashed it against the floor. The chair splintered into several parts. "I'll use this leg," Max said, picking up a part that had not broken. "It'll make a dandy lever."

"Max, you certainly are resourceful," 99 said admiringly. "I never would have thought of breaking that chair and using a leg to pry with. That was very clever."

"Your frankness is appreciated, 99," Max said. "But, actually, it was the most obvious thing to do. Anybody who's ever seen a western movie knows that these chairs crack up at almost the slightest touch." He inserted an end of the chair leg into the crack, then put his weight on the other end. There was a splintering sound and the leg snapped in two. "Just as I said—'crack up at the slightest touch,'" Max said. He tossed the broken chair leg aside. "Any other clever ideas, 99?" he asked sarcastically.

"Max, that was—"

"Save it," Max broke in. "You've used up your quota of frankness for today, 99." He walked over to a table and kicked a leg. The leg broke off. Max picked it up and examined it closely. "I think this will work a little better," he said. He lifted it over his head and smashed it against the floor. Again, there was a splintering sound. Max had smashed a large hole in the floor. "It just proves that the old adage is right," he said, returning to where 99 and the mule were standing. "Never send a chair leg to do a table leg's job." He put the narrow end of the table leg into the crack, then pried. There was a creaking sound, then the floor board came loose. Max got down on his knees again.

"Is it there, Max?"

"Yes, 99, the eye is still here," Max replied, rising. He began putting the floor board back in place.

"Wasn't it the penny, Max?"

"It wasn't the penny, 99," Max answered, rising. "Now, let's see, where shall we look next?"

"Max, what was it you saw? You said you saw an eye, and then you—"

"99, at some time in the long history of this saloon, a lady lost a small hand mirror down that crack. Now, does that answer all your questions sufficiently?"

"You mean it was—"

"Yes, it was *my* eye!"

"Hee-haw!"

"What did he say, Max?"

"He said it was a natural mistake because, as he recalls, Coolidge had blue eyes, too. Now, are we going to stand around all morning discussing eyes or are we going to look for that Coolidge-head penny?" He moved to a crack near the tables and inserted an end of the table leg and applied leverage. The floor board popped up. Again, Max got down on his knees.

99 and the mule had joined him. "What do you see this time, Max?" 99 asked.

"Something shiny like a penny!"

"It's it!" 99 cried.

"But I can't reach it," Max said. He plunged his whole arm into the hole. "It's— I don't know . . . I can't figure it out." He extracted his arm and stood up. "Look for yourself, 99," he said.

99 bent over and peered into the hole. "I see it!" she said. "You're right, Max, it's too far down to reach. I wonder what— Max! That's the basement!"

"I hardly think so, 99," Max said. "Remember where we are? We're in a saloon. If anything, that's a wine cellar down there."

"All right, Max. A basement, a wine cellar, what's the difference?"

"99, a wine cellar is a place where wine is kept. A cellar is a place that floods in spring. You'd know the difference, all right, if you kept your wine in the basement and it got water in it." He put the floor board back in place. "All we have to do now," he said, "is find the basement door."

"The basement door, Max?"

"How else do you think you get to the wine cellar, 99? You go down through the basement doorway." He walked to the rear of the saloon and entered the back room. When 99 and the mule joined him, he said, "Doesn't this remind you of the old song, 99?"

" 'Dead In the Baggage Coach Ahead,' Max?" 99 replied. "I don't see the connection."

"I meant the old song, 'See What the Boys in the Back Room Will Have,' " Max explained. He looked puzzled. "There's no basement door in here," he said. "And I didn't see one out in the other room, either. Where do you suppose the entrance to the basement is?"

"Wine cellar, you mean, Max."

"Basement, wine cellar—what's the difference." Max left the back room and returned to the main room, followed by 99 and the mule. He stopped and looked around again. "Maybe I'm looking for the wrong kind of door," he said. "Maybe you get to the wine cellar through a trapdoor. That makes sense. If the saloon-keeper had a lot of expensive wine stored in his wine cellar, he wouldn't have the door where anybody could see it. He'd hide it. He'd have. . . . Let me see . . . Of course! He'd have a trapdoor behind the bar."

With 99 and Madame DuBarry tagging along, Max hurried to the bar, then went behind it. "A secret trapdoor," he decided.

"What makes you think that, Max?"

"Do you *see* the trapdoor, 99?"

"No."

"Well, I don't either. So it must be a *secret* trapdoor. A little logic, 99, can be very helpful in answer-

ing those unanswerable questions." He began stomping
noisily on the floor. "I'll know when I find it because
I'll hear a hollow sound," he explained. "A little logic,
that's all it takes."

"I don't hear a hollow sound, Max."

"99, I'm only halfway to the end of the bar."

A short while later, Max reached the end.

"I didn't hear any hollow sound, Max."

"Hee-haw!"

"You can keep your comments to yourself, if you
don't mind," Max said crankily to the mule.

"What did he say, Max?"

"He said, 'Hee-haw!' He was giving me the old mule
laugh," Max replied. Once more, he looked around the
saloon. "Well, if the wine cellar isn't reached by trapdoor, then you must get to it by secret panel," he said.
"Logically, that's the only sensible answer." He walked
out from behind the bar and went to a wall and began
pressing the panels. "If I can just locate the right spot,
the panel will swing open, revealing the entrance to the
wine cellar. All these old castles have secret panels. I
think—"

"Max, this isn't an old castle," 99 pointed out. "It's
an old saloon."

"Old castle, old saloon—what's the difference. As
long as—"

"Hee-haw!"

"What?" Max asked. "I didn't get that."

"Max!" 99 cried. "He disappeared again!"

Reluctantly, Max took his attention from the wall.
He looked for the mule. "You're right, 99! He found
it!" he said.

"Found what, Max?"

"The secret panel! You don't seem to know any
more about horror movies than you do about westerns,
99. In all the horror movies, there's always a beautiful
girl, and she's always alone in this mysterious room—a

library most of the time—and then there's always a scream and she disappears through a secret panel. That's exactly what's happened here!"

"Max, that mule isn't exactly a beautiful girl!"

"99, he probably *thinks* he is. Why else would he name himself Madame DuBarry?"

"But this isn't a mysterious room."

"Isn't a mysterious room? 99, a mule who thinks he's a beautiful girl has just disappeared through a secret panel, and you don't think that's mysterious? What does it take?"

"All right, Max," 99 said. "A beautiful girl just screamed and then disappeared through a secret panel. But, where is it?"

"I don't know, 99," Max replied. "But now that we know for sure that it's here, we shouldn't have any trouble finding it. Where was the mule standing when he disappeared?"

"Right here beside me in the middle of the saloon, Max."

Max walked to the spot that 99 had pointed out and looked down at the floor. "Fantastic!" he said. "I could have wasted the whole day examining the walls in here, and all the time the secret panel would be here in the floor. The man who thought this up was a genius. Either that or he'd never seen any horror movies and didn't know where secret panels belong."

"He certainly did a great job of hiding it, though," 99 said. "That looks exactly like bare floor to me, Max."

"To me, too."

"Max, isn't it possible that the mule just disappeared—the way he did before."

"That would be too much of a coincidence, 99," Max replied. He began stomping on the floor. "Hear that! Does that sound hollow to you, 99?"

"No, Max."

"Mmmmmm . . . it doesn't sound hollow to me, either. It sounds more like—"

"It sounds like a noisy neighbor!" a voice said.

Max and 99 turned toward the sound of the voice. They found Arbuthnot and the other assassins standing in the entrance doorway. Arbuthnot had a pistol pointed at them.

"A noisy neighbor?" Max asked.

"Yes!" Arbuthnot replied, furious. "How do you expect us to hold a meeting over in the bank with you doing all that stomping over here in the saloon! You've made a mess of the whole morning, Smart! I was right in the middle of my lecture on 'Safe-Cracking—A Moral Confrontation with the Establishment,' when suddenly I was interrupted by a terrible racket that sounded like stomping. I sent one of my men out to see what was causing it. But just as he was leaving the bank, the noise stopped."

"I'd failed to find the trapdoor," Max explained.

"Then, next, right in the middle of my lecture on 'Getting a Good Night's Sleep and Having a Nourishing Breakfast Before an Assassination,' the stomping started again."

"I was looking for the secret panel in the floor," Max told him.

"Well, you ruined my whole morning!"

"I'm sorry, I'm sorry."

Arbuthnot looked at him narrowly. "You were looking for a secret panel on the floor? And a trapdoor? Why?"

"Oh. Well, I, uh . . . That's my hobby. Some people play with electric trains and some people save stamps and some people look for secret panels and trapdoors."

Arbuthnot looked down at the floor. He moved further into the saloon, then stomped. "It's solid," he said. "What's supposed to be under there?"

"Nothing. Absolutely nothing. If you're hooked on looking for trapdoors and secret panels, you don't care where they lead," Max said. "The kick is in finding them. As a matter of fact, if you find one that leads somewhere, you're usually disappointed. Because you have to follow it and find out where it leads to, and that gives you less time to go look for another trapdoor or secret panel."

"Smart, I don't believe you," Arbuthnot said. He moved to another stop—a place near the tables—and stomped again. "Aha!" he said. "It's hollow underneath."

"You're probably over the wine cellar," Max said.

"Oh . . . yes . . ." Arbuthnot replied, looking disappointed. He shrugged. "All right, Smart, don't tell me why you were doing all that stomping," he said. "It doesn't make any difference. I'm going to lock you up again. And, this time, I'm sure you won't get free. I won't make the mistake of sending food to you again. I've learned my lesson. Kindness doesn't pay."

"I think you mean 'Crime doesn't—'" Max began. Then he interrupted himself, and, after a second of looking thoughtful, he said, "I guess, in this case, at least, you're probably right."

Arbuthnot gestured toward the doorway. "Out!" he commanded.

"Back to the jail, eh?" Max said.

"Not this time," Arbuthnot replied. "I have a surprise for you. Out the door, then turn right toward the bank."

Max and 99 marched out of the saloon, followed by Arbuthnot. When they reached the porch, they headed for the bank. The other assassins joined Arbuthnot, tagging after them.

"I'm sorry, 99," Max said. "All this could have been avoided if I hadn't done that stomping."

"In the final analysis, it wasn't the stomping that led me to you," Arbuthnot told Max.

"Oh?"

"No. When the stomping started the second time, I sent my man out again. But just as he got outside, the stomping stopped—the way it had the first time."

"That was when I decided there wasn't a secret panel in the floor," Max said.

"Anyway, my man cane back," Arbuthnot went on. "He didn't know where the stomping sound was coming from. I didn't want to be interrupted again, though. So, my men and I left the bank and began an investigation, hoping to learn where the stomping sounds were coming from."

"That's logical enough," Max said. "But what was it that ultimately led you to us."

"I'd rather not say," Arbuthnot replied.

"Ah, come on."

"You won't believe it."

"Sure, I will. Promise. Cross my heart and etc., etc."

"Well . . . we followed what appeared to be drunken jack rabbit tracks," Arbuthnot said sheepishly.

8.

"Inside," Arbuthnot said, when they reached the bank.

"If you think you can buy us off—"

"Inside!" Arbuthnot repeated, prodding Max with the gun this time.

Max and 99 stepped through the entrance into the bank. One of the KAOS agents drew out a spray bottle and disinfected the doorway. Then Arbuthnot and all the KAOS assassins followed Max and 99 into the bank.

"If you think you can buy us off—" Max began once more.

"Back to the vault!" Arbuthnot ordered, waving the pistol.

Max led the way toward the rear of the bank. "A vault!" he whispered to 99. "Arbuthnot must have millions with him if he has to keep it in something as big as a vault. Maybe we ought to give bribery some second thoughts, 99. I mean, what's so terrible about accepting a little gift of money in return for doing an enemy a favor?"

"Max! It's dishonest!"

"No more dishonest than taking a company stamp to mail a letter, 99," he whispered. "If I do that, why shouldn't I accept a few million dollars from Arbuthnot as a bribe? We could look at it as a six-cent stamp."

"Max, I'm not sure—"

"Halt!" Arbuthnot commanded. He pointed to the door of the vault, which was closed. "There you are . . . that's for you," he said to Max.

"Sorry," Max replied. "According to my wife, we cannot be bribed." He stepped a few paces closer to Arbuthnot and lowered his voice. "However—"

"Bribed?" Arbuthnot said. "I have no intention of trying to bribe you. And—" He stepped back, looking bothered. "—don't get so close! I don't want your germs. I could get your Control germs and pass them on to other KAOS agents and start another epidemic as terrible as the bubonic plague." He issued an order to the KAOS agent with the spray bottle. "Get him!" he said, indicating Max.

The KAOS agent stepped forward and sprayed Max thoroughly.

"That was very exhilerating," Max said, waving away the mist of disinfectant. "But it didn't help your cause any," he said to Arbuthnot. "Before, you had a teensy-weensy chance of bribing me. You lost that chance, however, with that crack about Control and the bubonic plague."

"What gave you the idea I would try to bribe you?" Arbuthnot asked.

"That's a vault, isn't it?" Max said, pointing. "And it's a vault in a bank, isn't it? I just put two and two together, that's all. I have a very logical mind."

"Well . . . you're right—it *is* a vault, and it *is* in a bank," Arbuthnot said. "But I wasn't thinking about bribery. I had in mind a gift."

Max brightened. " A gift?"

"I think we owe you something," Arbuthnot said. "You've been quite entertaining. And cheap."

Max frowned. "I don't think I quite understand that."

"There's an old saying," Arbuthnot said. "It goes: All work and no play makes a KAOS assassin a little edgy before he has his morning coffee. That could have happened here. After all, this was a working meeting. And there are no night clubs and no movie houses in this ghost town. And all you can get on television are ghosts. So, we all could have become quite nudgy."

"Yes, I can see—"

"Thanks to you, however, we're all in good spirits," Arbuthnot said. He smiled. "See? I smiled. That proves that we're in good spirits." He turned to the other assassins. "Smile!" he ordered.

They smiled.

"Thanks to you—as you can see—we are all smiling," Arbuthnot said, facing Max again.

"I can see that," Max nodded, looking perplexed. "But how did I manage it?"

"You entertained us," Arbuthnot replied. "Your stupid, bumbling, idiotic attempts to overcome us were hilarious. We laughed our heads off." He turned to the other assassins again. "Show him how we laughed our heads off," he commanded.

The assassins doubled over with uncontrollable laughter.

"Cut!" Arbuthnot ordered.

The laughter immediately ceased.

"You see how we laughed our heads off," Arbuthnot said to Max. "You've been just what we needed to get our minds off our work after a long session of concentrated study. You're a great clown, Smart—the perfect fool."

"Perfect, yes," Max replied, mildly hurt. "Fool, no. This case isn't exactly closed yet, Arbuthnot. Before it's over, you may lose your heads from something besides laughing."

"Oh? You don't want the gift, then?"

"Well . . ." Max looked toward the vault. "We all like to be appreciated, even if it's for the wrong reason."

"Good, good," Arbuthnot smiled. "And I suppose you will want to share the gift with your fellow agent —your partner and wife."

"Yes," Max answered. "I think I ought to correct you on one point, however," he said. "She *is* my partner and wife. But she is not my fellow agent. I'd look pretty silly married to a fellow, wouldn't I?"

"Of course," Arbuthnot replied. "On the other hand, though, you look silly married to a woman, too. Who you are married to has nothing to do with it, however. The problem arises because of the fact that, married or single, you are silly-looking."

"Could we skip the rest of the build-up and get on to the gift-giving," Max said.

"Of course," Arbuthnot replied. "Mr. and Mrs. Smart . . . Agents 86 and 99 . . . it is my pleasure to present to you this bank vault. It will be your new home. And you will live in it as long as you live."

"Oh, Max!" 99 cried. "He's going to lock us in the vault!"

"Now, don't panic, 99. He didn't say that. Not exactly." Max turned to Arbuthnot. "Could you kind of . . . What I mean is, I don't—"

"I'm going to lock you in the vault," Arbuthnot explained.

"I was afraid of that. And you call that a gift? What kind of a gift is that?"

"A gift assassination," Arbuthnot replied. "It's what we do best."

"Oh." Max smiled thinly. "Oh . . . well, I suppose ·. . . yes, I can see the thought behind it . . . In a way, I guess, it's kind of sweet . . . in a sort of diabolical sort of way. . . . I wonder if it would do any good to yell HELP in this ghost town, way out here miles from civilization?"

"The cry wouldn't even get past the door of the vault," Arbuthnot informed him.

"Then we won't waste time on that," Max said. "We can go directly to the last resort—a screaming, kicking tantrum."

"That won't do any good, either," Arbuthnot told him. "That vault was built to withstand any force—dynamite, earthquakes, or the steady erosion of cellular structure caused by vibration." He motioned to Max and 99 with the gun. "Inside the vault, please."

A KAOS assassin opened the door of the vault, then Max and 99 entered. With only two of them inside, the vault was fairly roomy.

"Don't do anything I wouldn't do," Arbuthnot chuckled.

"Just a min—"

But Arbuthnot refused to listen. He signalled and a KAOS assassin slammed the door shut.

The interior of the vault was totally dark.

"Oh, Max!" 99 wailed. "What are we going to do?"

"I don't know, 99," Max said disgustedly. "That's what I wanted to talk to Arbuthnot about. He told us not to do anything he wouldn't do. But I'm not sure what that includes. If we'd only got to know him better, so that we could have noted some of his idiosyncrasies and crotchets. Then, with a better knowledge of his personality, we'd be able to make a more educated guess as to what he would do and wouldn't do."

"Max," 99 said, "I have the feeling that we got well enough acquainted with Arbuthnot to know that the only thing he *wouldn't* do is sleep in the same bed as a germ."

"That gives us a pret-ty wide leeway, 99. Because I got a glimpse of the interior of this vault before that KAOS assassin closed the door, and, although it's well equipped with empty shelves, the one thing it doesn't have is a bed. Keeping that in mind, I think we can use any means of escape we can work out without running the risk of offending our host."

"Max! Why should we worry about offending Arbuthnot?"

"99, after all, this vault *is* a gift!"

"But, Max, for heaven's—"

99 and Max were suddenly shoved against opposite walls of the vault.

"Max—what happened!" 99 cried.

"I can only guess, 99," Max replied. "What I do know, though, is that there is a large hairy body between us. And it has . . . let me see . . . two rather long ears . . . and one, two, three, four legs . . . and a tail that—"

"Hee-haw!"

"Sorry about that," Max apologized. To 99, he said, "I think it's a mule. In this darkness, I can't be positive, of course, but indications are that Madame DuBarry has reappeared—and just when we didn't need her most."

"Max . . . I can hardly move . . ."

"Madame," Max said to the mule, "you could be a lot more help if you went back to the saloon and continued to look for that secret panel that leads to the secret passageway to the wine cellar. If we don't find that Coolidge-head penny and signal the Chief, these KAOS assassins will get away."

"And, incidentally, we'll die in this vault," 99 added.

"Let's not worry about that, 99," Max said. "I don't

think we'll have any trouble getting out of the vault. The only reason I haven't broken out, so far, is that I want to be sure the KAOS assassins aren't still hanging around."

"Max!" 99 said, delighted. "You mean you really know how we can get out of here?"

"It's as simple as one-two-three, 99," he replied. "Or, at least, it will be as soon as we get rid of this mule. Madame DuBarry, would you mind moving over a step? You're standing on my foot."

"Hee-haw!"

"What did he say, Max?"

"He said I started it—I stood on his foot first."

"Max, tell him to leave."

"He's a guest, 99."

"I don't care. Our lives depend on it. You said you can't get us out of here until he leaves. If he's any kind of a friend at all, he'll vamoose."

"Hee-haw!"

"What did he say, Max?"

"Do you want all of the details or just the gist of it?"

"The gist will do."

"He said it's not that simple, 99. He has the same trouble with disappearing and reappearing as the old prospector has. He says he was gone the whole winter of '61, too. And, what was worse, he says, while the old prospector got to spend that winter in Miami Beach, he, Madame DuBarry, spent it in an abandoned igloo on a runaway ice floe in the Bering Strait."

"Max . . . he said all *that* with 'Hee-haw?'"

"It's the inflection he puts on the 'haw' that does it 99."

99 sighed wearily. "Max, why don't you try to get us out of here even though the mule is in with us? If

your plan is as simple as one-two-three, what difference will it make whether the mule is here or not?"

"Quite a bit of difference, 99," Max replied. "Because, my plan is to count 'one-two-three' and then
run and throw my weight against the door of the vault.
And it's next to impossible to run and throw your
weight against the door of a vault when you're pinned
against the wall by a mule."

"Oh, Max!" 99 moaned. "You mean that's really
your plan? To break down the door of the vault by
throwing your weight against it? Max, that won't do
any good at all. Didn't you hear what Arbuthnot said?
He said this vault could withstand the force of dynamite and an earthquake and severe vibration and almost anything!"

"I heard him, 99. And he probably thought he was
being entirely truthful. Just because he's an assassin,
that doesn't mean he's a fibber, too. Some of history's
most honest men have had other flaws in their characters. So, in all fairness, let's not assume that Arbuthnot
was lying. Let's just assume that he made a hasty judgment."

"Meaning what, Max?"

"99, I have no doubt at all that when this vault was
constructed it was built to withstand the force of dynamite, an earthquake or severe vibration or almost anything. But, 99, this vault, now, is centuries old."

"A century is a hundred years, Max."

"Decades old?"

"That's more like it, Max. But, I don't see— Oh.
You mean you think it's not as strong as it used to
be?"

"Did you see the hinges on that door, 99? I could pry
those hinges off with a toothpick. All I have to do is
throw my weight against that door once and it will go
flying right out of the bank. Now, if Madame DuBarry

would just leave, so I could back off and get a good running start . . ."

"Max . . . I have sort of an idea . . . Madame DuBarry is facing the back of the vault. So, that means his heels are near the door."

"Which heels, 99? He has four, you know."

"His hind heels, Max. In other words, his kicking heels. So, why can't he kick down the door for us?"

"99, that's an excellent idea. Frankly, it's the kind of idea I usually get. Now, let's see what the mule thinks of it. Madame DuBarry, an idea has just occurred to me. Suppose—"

"Hee-haw!"

"What did he say, Max?"

"In addition to the crack about people who try to take credit for other people's ideas, you mean? Well, he said it's an excellent idea. And he's going to— He's doing it now, 99!"

"Yes . . . I can— Oh, Max!"

"It could happen to anybody, 99. His timing was off, that's all."

"I felt him rear up to kick, and then—poof!"

"I just hope he didn't end up on that runaway ice floe in the Bering Strait again," Max said. "His disappearance won't hamper us any, though, 99. Now, I have room to back off and get that running start and knock that door down. I'll just get down here at this far end . . ."

"Careful, Max . . ."

"Stay flattened against the wall, 99," Max said. "I can't see you in this darkness, and I don't want to run into you."

"I'm out of the way, Max."

"Then . . . here I go! One-two-three—!"

A second later there was a thud. Then silence.

"Max? Max . . . are you all right? Max . . . where are you, Max?"

"I-I-I-I'm st-t-t-t-t-ill here, 9-9-9-9-9."

"Max, why do you sound so strange?"

"I-I-I-I'm st-t-t-t-t-ill vibrat-t-t-t-t-ing, 99."

"I guess the door isn't as weak as it looks, right, Max?"

"Right, 99," Max replied. "But that doesn't mean I can't break it down. I'll just have to keep charging it, that's all. A few more times and those hinges will snap and that door will go flying. All right . . . stay back against the wall, 99. I'm going to try it again."

"Max, maybe you better not."

"Don't stop me when I'm winning, 99. One-two-three—go!"

A second passed, then the thud was heard once more.

"Max?"

"If at first you don't succeed, so forth and so forth and so forth, 99. Just stay back out of the way. One-two-three—Go!"

Thud!

"One . . . uh, two . . . three—Go!"

Thud!

"One . . . one and a half . . . two . . . two and a half . . . two and three quarters . . . three—go."

Thud.

"Max?"

"99 . . . I'd rather not discuss it. I'm broken in body and spirit."

"You just need a rest, Max. Take time out, then try it again."

"Yes . . . I'll just lean against the back of the—"

There was a crash. Light suddenly flooded into the vault. Blinking, 99 saw Max lying outside on the floor, on top of the rear wall.

"Max . . . what happened?" she asked, baffled.

"When I leaned against the back wall of the vault,

99, it fell out. The whole vault, apparently, is about to crumble."

"Except for the hinges," 99 said.

"Except for the hinges," Max nodded, rising. He looked around. "Well, there are no KAOS assassins hanging around. So, I guess we can get back to the saloon and look for that Coolidge-head penny." He headed for the door. "Come on, 99. Let's get over to the saloon and find that penny before this seminar ends and all those KAOS assassins get away."

"Right behind you, Max!"

Max reached the door—and abruptly halted. 99 crashed into him.

"Max!"

"Back, 99!" he said. He retreated, then peeked out the doorway. "Talk about terrible luck!" he said. "Look! All the KAOS assassins are trooping into the saloon!"

"Yes!" 99 groaned. "I wonder why they're going in there?"

"Arbuthnot is probably going to instruct them on How to Cheat at Poker While Assassinating the Bartender," Max said.

"That's the last of the assassins—they're all inside the saloon," 99 said. "What shall we do now, Max?"

"Somehow, we have to get them out of there, so we can search for the secret panel that leads to the secret passageway that leads to the wine cellar, where we can begin looking for the Coolidge-head penny."

"Max . . . have you noticed how complicated this is getting?"

"I don't know why that surprises you, 99. It was bound to get more and more complicated. I'm surprised, frankly, that it isn't more complicated than it is."

"Why is that, Max?"

"Well, you know what they say. The best things are

the simple things. So, the worst things must be the complicated things. And what could be worse than this?"

"I see what you mean, Max."

"Let's sneak up on the saloon and listen at one of the windows," Max said. "Maybe we'll hear something that will give us an idea how we can get those assassins out of there." Cautiously, he moved out the door. "Quiet, 99," he warned. "Don't make a sound." He halted. "And, Madame DuBarry, if you're with us, that goes for you, too."

"Hee-Haw!" a familiar voice responded.

"Shhhhhhhhh!"

Silently, Max, 99, and possibly the mule, slipped out of the bank and crossed the dusty street to the saloon. When they reached a window, Max and 99 bent low, keeping out of sight, and listened. Madame DuBarry, if he was present, had no need to bend down.

Arbuthnot was telling the other assassins how pleased he was with the way they had responded to instruction.

"I'll be honest with you," he said. "When I first took a look at you, I said to myself, 'What a bunch of dumbheads!' But I was wrong. Each one of you is an individual. You're not a 'bunch' to me any more. You're all dumb in your own stupid personal way."

"The typical farewell address," Max said, bored. "We're not going to learn anything here, 99."

"Shhhhh—just listen, Max."

"But, dumb as you are, with me as your professor, you *had* to learn something," Arbuthnot went on. "I venture to say that from now on you'll all think twice before you pick up a weapon to go out to assassinate somebody. You'll remember what I told you about germs. The phrase 'kill, kill, kill' will now have an added meaning. Before you assassinate the victim, you'll assassinate those dirty germs! And you'll all be better assassins for it—not to mention your victims, who will die the right way—by knife, gun or poison— instead of by accident from getting your dirty, filthy old germs!"

"Well, maybe not completely typical," Max said. "But, even so, 99, we're not learning anything that can help us. Let's get out of here before we're spotted."

"All right, Max."

They crept away and returned to the bank.

"Did you think of anything, Max?" 99 asked. "How are we going to get them out of the saloon?"

"I'm sorry, 99, but I wasn't thinking about that at all," Max replied. "The truth is, my mind was wandering. That always happens to me when I listen to speeches. I was listening to Franklin D. Roosevelt in December, 1941, when he announced that the Japanese had attacked Pearl Harbor, but I didn't find out about it until January, 1942, at a New Year's Eve party. While he was announcing Pearl Harbor, I was thinking about maraschino cherries. I was calculating exactly how long it would take a maraschino cherry weighing one ounce to sink one inch into a mound of whipped cream six inches high if the whipped cream had a stable consistency of— Well, anyway, you probably get the idea."

"Max, what were you thinking about while you were supposed to be listening to Arbuthnot's farewell speech?"

"I was thinking that probably the reason why we didn't find that secret panel that led to the secret passageway that led to the wine cellar that the Coolidge-head penny dropped into was because there isn't any

secret panel that leads to a secret passageway that
leads to— Well, anyway, you probably get the idea."

"But, Max, we saw the cellar. And we saw the
Coolidge-head penny. At least, you said we saw them."

"We did see the penny, 99," Max nodded. "But I
was mistaken about the cellar, I think. I think what we
really saw was the lost gold mine."

"Max, I don't understand."

"99, where is a mine?"

"Where is-a yours? Max, I don't even-a know-a
where-a mine is, let-a alone-a yours."

"You're very good on dialect, 99. But what I meant
was, where are mines usually located?"

"Oh. Underground, Max."

"Right. So, what was it we saw when we looked
down that crack in the floor? We saw the mine tunnel.
That explains why we couldn't find the secret panel
that led to the secret passageway that led to the wine
cellar. No secret panel, no secret passageway, and no
wine cellar. Only a mine tunnel. And that's where the
Coolidge-head penny is."

"Then we ought to be searching the mine!"

"Right again, 99."

"Of course!" 99 said. "Why didn't we think of that
before!"

"I don't know about you, 99," Max replied, leading
the way from the bank, "but the reason I didn't think
of it was because Arbuthnot hadn't got around to giving his farewell speech yet."

9.

MAX AND 99 STARTED UP the dusty street toward the mine. But after they had gone a few steps, Max halted. "We're making the same mistake we made last time," he said to 99, pointing to the tracks they were leaving in the dust. "When Arbuthnot and those other assassins came out of the saloon, they'll see our tracks and follow us up to the mine."

"I don't see how we can help but leave tracks, Max," 99 said. "There's dust all around."

"Only on the ground," Max said. "Not inside the buildings, and not on the roofs."

"Well . . . I suppose not, but—"

"Just follow me," Max said.

With 99 right behind him, Max entered the bakery. He ducked down and crawled into the old open fireplace, then, with excruciating slowness, he made his way up to the inside of the chimney. When he reached the roof he reached down and gave 99 a hand, helping her out.

"Max . . ." she panted, "I never thought I'd make it. Is this really necessary?"

117

"This is only the beginning, 99."

Max crossed to the edge of the roof. The roof of the next building, the jail, was several yards away. He retreated, then got a running start and leaped off the bakery roof and—with the tips of his fingers—caught hold of the drain pipe alone the edge of the jail roof. Summoning all his strength, Max pulled himself up, finally reaching the roof over the jail.

"Jump, 99!" he called.

"Max, I'll never make it!"

"It's the only way! Jump!"

99 backed away, then ran toward the edge of the bakery roof and jumped. She missed the edge of the jail roof—and the hands Max was holding out to her—by at least a foot, and plummeted to the ground, landing, fortunately, in a soft pile of dust.

"Oh, Max . . . I'm sorry . . ." 99 called up.

"You're forgiven, 99. Now, back into the bakery, and back up the chimney, and try it again. If at first you don't succeed, try—"

"Max, are you going into the jail?"

"No, 99. I'm going to cross to the roof of the lumber yard, then, by plank, make my way to the barber shop. Having retained the plank, I will then proceed to the roof of the bakery, reaching it by climbing hand-over-hand up the treacherous incline formed by extending the plank from the lower window of the barber shop to the upper gutter of the bakery roof. From the roof, I will drop down the chimney."

"Max, as long as I know where you're going, I'll just meet you outside the bakery."

"All right, 99."

Max disappeared from the edge of the roof. When he was gone, 99 walked around to the front of the bakery and saw down on the front steps. She heard a great deal of grunting and straining during the next few minutes. Then Max appeared from the bakery. His clothes were ripped in a number of places.

"That takes care of that problem," he said. "Arbuthnot and his assassins might, in time, be able to follow that trail. But a lot of them will probably lose their lives doing it. And, by the time they catch up with us, we'll have found the Coolidge-head penny and alerted the Chief."

"That's nice, Max," 99 said, managing to control her admiration.

"Now, 99—to the mine."

"Fine, Max."

They left the bakery and proceeded up the dusty street, leaving a full set of tracks behind. When they reached the entrance to the mine, they stopped and peered, squinting, into the darkness.

"Do you still have your lighter, Max?" 99 said. "We'll sure need it. I just wonder how long it will keep burning, though. I wouldn't want to get lost in there without a light."

"99, there's no problem. Even without a light we'd be able to find our way out. Tunnels only go two ways —out and in. If we came to the end of the tunnel and discovered that we weren't outside, we'd know we were going the wrong way. So, we'd turn around and go the other way, which would take us out."

"Suppose the tunnel has branches, Max?"

"We'll stay *out* of the branches. This is no time to go out on a limb." Max reached into his pocket to get the lighter. "I don't seem to have it," he said. "Did I give the lighter to you, 99?"

"I don't think so, Max."

"We'll just have to go on without it," he decided. "We don't really need it. We'll see the Coolidge-head penny when we reach it. Remember?—it was gleaming in the light through the crack in the floor."

"But, Max—"

"It's just as well that I can't find the lighter, 99," Max said. "If I lit it the flame would cast flickering shadows on the walls. And when a flame casts a flickering shadow on the walls that means that danger is lurking somewhere nearby. It's a warning the Good Guys always get."

"Max . . . you don't really believe that, do you?"

"Why wouldn't I believe it, 99? It never fails to happen. When a candle or a lighter is lighted in a dark place like a cave or a tunnel, the flame always flickers. And then, a short while later, the danger always comes out of lurking and confronts the Good Guys."

"But, Max, that's the wind blowing the flame!"

"If you want to think it's the wind, 99, that's your privilege."

"What is it, then?"

"It's the sacred god of Good Guydom."

"Oh, Max, you can't—"

There was a sudden sound, like a puff of air, and the old prospector suddenly appeared. He was carrying his lantern and blocking the way. Beside him was his mule, Madame DuBarry.

"Well . . . speak of the god of Good Guydom . . ." Max said.

"None of your soft soap!" the old prospector growled. "I caught you red-handed this time!"

Max looked at his hands. "That's not my normal color," he said. "They're getting the reflection from your lantern."

"None of your squirmy way with words, either! You know what I'm talking about!" the old prospector charged. "You're after my gold! You had me fooled at first with that story about the Pinkertons. But now I've got the goods on you. If you're not after my gold, what are you doing back in the tunnel?"

"It's sort of a long story," Max said. "After you disappeared and left us stranded on that mountain, we made our way down to the town, and, at the break of dawn, found ourselves confronted——"

"Don't go into all that detail," the old prospector said. "I disappeared, all right, but that don't mean I haven't kept track of you. I been on your trail every minute of the time—almost. I had my suspicions, so I followed you—staying about a dozen yards behind. I saw you get yourself trapped in that jail. I saw you get shut up in that vault in the bank. The only place I didn't tail you was when you jumped over from the roof of the bakery to the roof of the jail."

"Oh? Chicken?"

"Well, I saw your wife take that fall. So, I said to myself—Well, never mind what I said. What it adds up to is, yeah, I was chicken. I went along with her and waited on the porch."

"I see. Well, if you've been with us all the time, then you must know why we're here," Max said. "Didn't you hear us say why we were returning to the tunnel?"

"From a dozen yards behind?" the old prospector replied. "I didn't have ears like that even when I was young."

"Oh. Well, if you'd been a little closer," Max said, "you'd have heard us say—very clearly—that we were coming back here to look for the Coolidge-head penny. You see, our idea that the penny dropped through the floor and into the wine cellar was wrong. Because there is no wine cellar below the saloon. What there is, instead, is a tunnel. A mine tunnel. *This* mine tunnel. And that's why we're here now. To find the Coolidge-head penny, not to look for your gold. I hope that clears up any misunderstanding that may have arisen. Are you satisfied?"

"Almost," the old prospector replied. "I will be as soon as I take care of you two so you can't get at my gold."

"Apparently I'm going to have to start at the beginning again," Max said wearily. "It all started, you see, in Washington. Now, 99 and I—"

"Max, we don't have time for that!" 99 said. "If Arbuthnot was giving a farewell speech, he and the other assassins will be leaving soon."

"You're right, 99," Max replied. He addressed the old prospector again. "I'll explain it afterwards," he said. "But, right now—" He pointed. "See that lantern hanging on the wall," he said. "I'm going to take it and light it and then follow this tunnel until I find the Coolidge-head penny. I promise that if I find any gold—"

"Don't do that," the old prospector warned.

"Max, you can't do it, anyway," 99 said. "You lost the lighter."

"I just found it again a second ago, 99," he replied. "It was in my other pocket all the time."

"Then, quick, Max, let's hurry."

"Sorry old man," Max said to the old prospector, getting the lighter from his pocket.

"It's not me that'll be sorry," the old prospector said. "It's you that'll be—"

Max, having taken the lantern from the wall, ignited the lighter. There was a resounding explosion. It was followed by the sound of falling rocks.

"—sorry," the old prospector finished.

Max and 99 stared at the entrance to the tunnel, which was now blocked by huge stones.

"That exactly the way it happened to me," the old prospector told them. "I come in here with a lantern and when I started to light it I got this big boom. Then all them rocks come crashing down and clogged up the doorway."

"Max!" 99 cried. "We're trapped."

"My guess is there's a gas leak in here somewhere," the old prospector speculated.

"Just a minute," Max said. "We still have light.

Why is it that your lantern doesn't cause an explosion?"

" 'Cause it's not real," the old man replied. "What would a ghost prospector be doing with a real lantern? Don't you know a ghost lantern when you see one?"

"He's right, Max," 99 said.

"All right, he's right," Max said. "But, don't panic, 99. All we have to do is find the Coolidge-head penny and signal to the Chief. Then he'll send a squad of Control agents to capture the assassins, and after they've finished that they can free us."

"Ha!" the old prospector said.

"What exactly does that mean?" Max asked.

"It means it looks like it won't be long before I'm not the only human ghost in this here lost gold mine," the old prospector replied, grinning. "And, let me tell you, it'll be nice having you young folks around. Madame DuBarry is a good mule, but, no matter how you look at it, he's not human. I crave the company of human people. Oh, Madame DuBarry can be a good talker—if you can hit on a subject that interests him. But, after you've discussed the various aspects of straw a couple or six times, it's hard to find anything new to say about it. I'm truly looking forward to the chats I'll have with you two after you get to be ghosts. Why . . . we'll recollect old times. I can tell you how it was back in the days when a man was a man and a woman was glad of it. And you can tell me how things was yesterday and the day before. Yessirree! We'll have many a good argyments, too. I remember the night I took on Hotfoot Luke in the bar of the saloon on the subject: Will the Iron Horse Ever Replace the Twenty Mule Team as the Primary Means of Trans-Continental Transportation. It was a debate like you've never heard the likes of before or since. Hotfoot Luke took the Affirmative. And I took both the Negative and the Maybe. I proved beyond a doubt that the Iron Horse was a rich man's toy and it'd never get off the ground. When I finished my summin' up, the roar of the crowd was deafening."

"Yes, well, as it happened, you were wrong, though," Max said. "The Iron Horse is still with us today, and it's still a very important part of the transportation system."

"Pshaw!" the old prospector said. "Where'd you ever get an idea like that? It didn't last a week. Like I said in the debate, it was a rich man's toy."

"It just so happens," Max replied, "that there are trains—"

"Trains? Who said anything about trains? I'm talking about the Iron Horse. It was invented by Abe Shuster, a rich fella here in town—before the town kind of petered out, that is. He had this idea for a machine that looked just like a horse. He got the local ironsmith to build it for him. Had an iron tail and iron ears. While he was at it, the ironsmith made up a whole bushel of iron corn for this iron horse to eat. But, I told them at the time, 'It'll never be anything but Abe Shuster's toy,' I said. And I was right. A couple days after the big debate—which I won hands down—that iron horse run off with the iron deer that Mabel Wamsutter had on her front lawn. Neither one was ever heard from or seen again."

"Well, that's very sad, but—"

"Sadder than that even," the old prospector said. "It was due to that—the coincident of his iron horse running off with her iron deer—that caused Abe Shuster to first take notice of Mabel Wamsutter, although they'd been living side by side—him in the big white house on the hill, and her in the little hovel in the valley—for nigh onto a good long while. The tragedy that resulted shook the whole town to its very roots. I recall—"

"Max," 99 said, "if we're going to find that Coolidge-head penny—"

"Just a second, 99. I want to find out what happened to Abe and Mabel."

"Max!"

"You're right, 99. Duty first," Max said.

"Sure, that's right, you go on ahead and waste your time looking for that penny," the old prospector said. "We'll talk about Abe and Mabel later. We'll have plenty of time after you're bona fide ghosts. Centuries and centuries and centuries. Maybe even a whole decade."

"Fine," Max nodded. "Now, if you'll just excuse ue . . ."

"Sure."

Max and 99 started off into the dimness.

"Just yell when you get hopelessly lost in one or more of them branch tunnels," the old prospector called after them.

Max and 99 returned.

"Branch tunnels?" Max said.

"Yup. Go on ahead if you want to go out on a limb and take a chance on getting lost in one of them branch tunnels," the old prospector said. "There're hundreds of them. More than that even. I counted up to a hundred, then I stopped counting. When you two get to be ghosts along with me and Madame DuBarry, maybe we'll take that up as a hobby—counting all them branch tunnels. Time hangs a little heavy on your hands when you're a ghost and you're haunting a long lost gold mine. I'll tell you the truth, you don't get much traffic through a long lost gold mine. A couple of Dairy Queen fellas stopped by here one day about a dozen years ago to survey the place and see if it'd pay to put up a stand. Well, they stood here and counted, both pedestrian passersby and mule teams, and after they'd counted up to zero they quit. That's how busy the place is."

"Why are there hundreds of branches?" Max asked.

"That long lost gold has been lost for a long time," the old man answered. "And every new prospector that looked for it struck out in a different direction. The old prospectors have an old saying. It goes: Never trust an old prospector. So, every time some new old prospector would come along to look for the long lost gold, he'd dig the opposite way the last old old prospector'd dug. And, after a time—"

"I think I get the idea," Max broke in. "Look, I wonder if we could make a deal with you? It seems that in order to avoid getting lost we'll need a light. It seems, further, that you are in possession at the moment of the only reliable means of illumination. Are you following me?"

"Into that dark? Not me. I'm going to stay back here with the lantern—even if it *isn't* real."

"What I was getting at is, I wonder if we could borrow your lantern?"

"You don't know any more about ghosts than you do about iron horses," the old prospector replied. "How can I loan you the borrow of my lantern if it isn't real? Oh, I could loan you the borrow of it, but how would you carry it? Wait a few days, though. Then, you'll be a ghost, too, and you won't have any trouble at all carrying it."

"By then, I won't need it," Max said.

"Could you do this?" 99 said to the old prospector. "Could you guide us? We can see fine as long as you're around with the lantern."

"Guide you?" the old prospector said. "I'd be a fool to do that. Why should I guide *you* to that long lost gold when I can't even find it myself? I might be dumb enough to strike a light around a gas leak, but I'm not so dumb as to guide a couple of complete strangers to a place I don't even know where it is myself. Try me again in a couple days—after we know each other a little better."

"You still don't understand!" 99 said woefully. "Honest, we're not after your gold. All we want is that Coolidge-head penny."

"You're wasting your time. I been in every tunnel in this mine—almost—and not once have I ever seen a Coolidge-head penny."

"We know that," Max said. "We only lost it a couple days ago."

"Please!" 99 begged.

"Wellllllll . . ." the old prospector said. "It'll take a little while for you to turn to ghosts. I suppose, just to kill a little time—if you'll pardon the expression—I could show you around the mine. You'll be interested in seeing where you'll be living—though, that's not exactly the word for it—the rest of your life—though, that's not the word for it, either." He motioned. "Come on." Then, followed by Madame DuBarry and Max and 99, he led the way deeper into the mine. "Now, on your right," he said, "you'll see a long scratch along the wall about belt buckle high. There's a very interesting story that goes with that scratch. It seems that one day—"

"You can just skip the commentary that goes along with the tour," Max said. "We'll be looking for the Coolidge-head penny, and we don't want to be distracted."

"Oh, there's no commentary," the old prospector said. "I just want you to hear about that scratch on the wall about belt buckle high. It's an interesting story, and you'd be after me to tell it to you sooner or later. This way, if I tell it to you now, you won't have to ask later. It seems there was this nosy old prospector who came wandering in here one day, looking for a long lost gold mine, more than likely, and what did he run

into but the ghost of the previous old prospector—him
and his mule and his lantern. Well, this trespassin' old
prospector got so all-fired scared that he didn't even
take time to turn around and run. No, sir. He only
took time to half-turn. And that put him facing the
wall. And that's how he run out, too—facing the wall.
That's how come that wall's got that long scratch on it
belt-buckle high. It was made by that old prospector's
belt buckle. Now, coming up on the left here, you'll
see an entrance to another tunnel. The history of the
mine would not be complete without the telling of the
story connected with this here tunnel. It has to do with
a love story. I recall the incident as clear as if it'd
only happened maybe twenty or thirty years go.
There was this rich old man that lived in a big white
house on the hill. He went by the initials of A. S. He
was the fella in the story. The girl in the story was a
woman that went by the initials of M. M. Well—"

"Her initials were M. W.," Max corrected.

"Yeah, that's right," the old prospector nodded. "I
have a little trouble remembering all the details, it happened so long ago. Be that as it may, though, this couple, this crazy old man that had his mind set on inven-
tin' the railroad steam engine, and this beautiful young
lady that lived in the hovel in the valley, they—" He
halted and looked questioningly at Max. "You know
this story, do you?" he said.

"No. But, frankly—"

"If you don't know it, how come you know it's
about Albert Senagalese and Marybelle Wastehanger?"

"I don't," Max replied. "I thought it was about Abe
Shuster and Mable Wamsutter."

"It is," the old prospector said. "You don't think I'd
use their right names, though, do you? We don't mention them around here any more—not since the tragedy."

"That's understandable, I suppose," Max said. He

pointed ahead. "That tunnel up there," he said, "have you ever explored in there? If my calculations are correct, that's the direction we should go to get to the spot under the saloon."

"The saloon is the other way," the old prospector said.

Max pointed in the opposite direction. "That way?"

The old prospector shook his head. "Nope—the *other* way."

Max pointed forward. *"That* way, you mean, then?"

"Keep trying," the old prospector said.

"The only other way is the way we just came," Max pointed out.

"Right. You go back to the entrance and, by superhuman strength, you move all them big rocks out of the way, then you walk back to town and just on the other side of the bakery you'll find—"

"Max, he's stalling!" 99 said. "He has no intention of trying to help us."

Max peered at the old prospector challengingly. "For your information," he informed him, "I happen to think you're trying to stall us. Furthermore, I'm beginning to suspect that you have no intention of trying to help us."

The old man sighed. "You seen through me like a brick wall," he said. "I confess—you're right. The truth is, it's been so long since I had anything like human company that I was just stringing you along to keep you from leaving. But, I can see it won't work any more. Why, a couple of young, handsome folks like you can't be expected to stand around in a dark and dank old mine and listen to an old prospector like myself run off at the memory for very long. You got things to do. You got corn to plant. You got ears to shuck. You got grain to grind. You got flour to bag. You got cakes to bake. You got icing to mix. You got coffee to brew. You got a sugar bowl to get down off the cupboard shelf. You got a cow to milk. You got—"

"A cow to milk?" Max broke in.

"Oh . . . you want that coffee black? I thought you'd take cream in it. But, in that case, you got—"

"Hold it!" Max broke in again. "Look, old prospector, we've wasted enough time. Unless you cooperate, I'm afraid I'm going to have to get nasty."

The old man glared at him. "You threatening me, boy?"

"That's exactly what I'm doing," Max said threateningly. "Either you cooperate, or I'm going to stop believing in you. Do you have any idea what happens to ghosts when people stop believing in them?"

The old prospector snapped to attention. "At your service, sir! Anything you want, sir! Where to, sir!"

10.

W ITH THE OLD PROSPECTOR and his mule guiding
them, Max and 99 explored tunnel after tunnel. They
found a number of things. They found all the instru-
ments of a brass band that had marched into a tunnel
and had been unable to get out because it had never
learned to march backwards. They found the remains
of a newsreel photographer who had entered a tunnel
to film the remains of a newsreel photographer who
had been trapped in the tunnel earlier. They found a
pile of old and young bones and near them, scratched
on the wall, the message: "All things considered, A.S.
is relatively fond of M.W., and vice versa." But they
did not find the Coolidge-head penny.

"How many more tunnels to search?" Max asked
the old prospector glumly.

"Depends," the old man replied. "Are we going to
stop with this mine or go on to other mines? There're
about a hundred, I reckon, in all, in them thar hills—
mines, that is. And every mine has about a hundred
tunnels, in all, I reckon. So, when you say, 'How
many—"

"In just this mine," Max broke in.

"Well, speaking in a general way, I'd say I couldn't say. I run across new tunnels almost every day. It wouldn't surprise me to discover that we've got a tunnel-laying chicken down here with us."

"Max, remember," 99 said, "Arbuthnot was making a farewell speech. We don't know how long those assassins will still be here. We better find out some way to eliminate some of these tunnels from our search."

"Old prospector," Max said to the old prospector, "when I saw that Coolidge-head penny it was shining in the light that reached it through the crack in the floor. Now, from down here, it seems to me, that penny would have a shaft of light beaming down on it from above. Can you recall ever seeing anything like that down here?"

The old prospector thought for a few minutes then shook his head. "No. But there are some dandy cave carvings on the wall of the tunnel that's next in line to search," he said. "Let's just mosy on and take a look at them. This one carving has been kind of a source of inspiration to me while I been down here. It's a How To. It shows in minute detail how to hitch a musk ox to a four-bladed plow. Why the insinuation in that carving—you wouldn't believe it. The fella that carved it must've had a mind like—"

"Will you concentrate on the Coolidge-head penny, please?" Max broke in. "Now, think again. There is a shaft of light. It penetrates the darkness like—"

"Don't waste your time," the old prospector said. "I been in every tunnel in this mine but one and I never seen anything like that in any of them."

"Oh. Well . . ."

"Max," 99 said, "if he's been in every tunnel but one and hasn't seen anything like that, then isn't it logical that perhaps it's in the one tunnel he hasn't been in?"

"Yes . . . that is logical, 99. After all, everybody knows that whatever you're looking for you always find it in the last place you look. So, instead of searching all these other tunnels, and then searching the last tunnel last, let's search the last tunnel now, and save all the others for later." He faced the old prospector again. "Where is this tunnel you've never been in?" he asked.

"We're in it," the old man replied.

Max looked around. "Oh, yes, I see—we're in the entrance to another tunnel. All right, this time, I'll lead the way. Onward!"

With Max in the lead and 99 right behind him they moved deeper into the tunnel.

"You won't find anything," the old prospector said. "If this tunnel was that important, I'd've been in here before. I've never been down this way because all I had to do was look at the entry and I could see it wasn't worth looking into. When you've been looking for long lost gold as long as I have, you get a feeling for that kind of thing. I can look at the entry to a tunnel and size it up in the wink of an eye. Why, I remember back in '89 when I'd only been in this tunnel a few—"

"Max!" 99 cried out. "Look! Ahead!"

"Where's a head?" the old prospector asked, maneuvering to see around Max and 99. "It's probably just the left-over from some newsreel photographer. I remember— By Golly!" he suddenly shouted, having finally caught a glimpse of what had attracted 99's attention. "It's it! It's my long lost gold!"

Several yards ahead, a shaft of light was shining down from above, focused on what appeared to be a huge pile of gold coins.

"Finders keepers!" the old prospector shouted. He rushed forward and dived head-first into the pile of gold, and began flinging coins in all directions, driven to a frenzy by elation.

"Did you see how he ran over there, 99," Max said. "That's what's known as a gold rush."

"I saw it, Max."

Max and 99 approached the spot where the old prospector was still celebrating his find. He was scooping up coins and letting them filter through his fingers, meanwhile crying, "Gold! Gold! Gold! Mine! Mine! Mine! Gold Mine! Gold Mine! Gold Mine!"

"He's a little excited," Max commented.

"I'm not surprised . . . after all these years," 99 replied. She picked up one of the coins. "It's funny how when they're not directly in the light these gold coins don't look as shiny and as much like— Max! Look at this!" She handed the coin to Max.

He peered at it closely. Then he picked up another coin and looked at it closely, too.

"Is it the same, Max?" 99 asked.

"Yes, 99. Pure copper. These aren't gold coins, they're copper coins. They only looked gold in the light. What the old prospector has found is a pile of pennies."

"Gold! Gold! Gold!" the old prospector was shouting. "All mine! Gold mine! All—" He suddenly interrupted himself and glared at Max. "What was that unpatriotic thing you just said?" he asked.

"Unpatriotic?"

"I don't think I like it," the old prospector said. "And if I don't like it, it's unpatriotic. Now, what was it?"

"All I said was—"

"Pennies!" the old prospector cried, appalled. He looked at the coins he was clutching in his hands. "You're right! Pennies! I've been wiped out! The whole round trip—from the big white house on the hill to the hovel in the valley—in the flick of an eyelash!

I'm a ruined man. Being a ghost, I can't even take comfort in the fact that I still got my health! Oh, woe!"

"Well, it's not really as bad as all that," Max said. "Even if it *had* turned out to be gold, where would you have spent it?"

"Over at the general store," the old prospector replied. "I could've bought myself a new lantern—a real one this time."

"Well, if it's any consolation," Max said, "you have the satisfaction of knowing that, although you didn't find the long lost gold, you did deliver us to our hoped-for-destination."

"It's no consolation," the old prospector said bitterly.

"And, as a consequence—"

"It's no satisfaction, neither," the old man added.

"Max," 99 said, "do you mean—"

"Yes, 99, we have found the Coolidge-head penny," Max informed her. He pointed upward. "Do you see where the shaft of light is coming from? It's coming from a crack in the ceiling. But if we were up there instead of down here that crack in the ceiling would be a crack in the floor."

"You're right, Max. That's a marvelous deduction."

"Your frankness is refreshing, 99. Now, taking the deduction a bit further, we learn that what appears to be a crack in the ceiling, but which is actually a crack in the floor, is, to be even more specific, a crack in the floor of the saloon. So, if we were able to rise up out of this mine, and go straight up, where would we find ourselves?"

"Back at them pearly gates," the old prospector said.

"I didn't have in mind going quite that far," Max said. "What I was trying to explain was that the saloon is directly overhead."

"A lot of good that'll do," the old man said. "You couldn't even reach it standing on a mule."

"That's correct," Max replied. "You're missing the important point, however. What is important is that if that is the saloon up above, and that crack in the ceiling is actually the crack in the saloon floor, and if the Coolidge-head penny dropped through the crack in the saloon floor and fell into a tunnel of the mine below, then all I have to do to retrieve the Coolidge-head penny is bend down and pick it up from. . . . oh, my, those pennies really are scattered around, aren't they?"

"Max," 99 said gloomily, "it could take us days or weeks or months to find that Coolidge-head penny."

"Even decades," the old prospector smiled.

"Where did all these pennies come from, Max?" 99 asked.

"Obviously, 99, they dropped through the crack in the floor in the saloon. Pennies have probably been dropping through that crack for dec— For a long time. Haven't you ever noticed, 99, that pennies always drop through the same crack? The next time you drop a penny and it falls down a crack, mention it to the next person you meet. He'll tell you that just the day before he lost a penny down that very same crack. It's the way the pennies are trained, I think. I've known of pennies to roll for miles just to fall down a certain crack." He looked around at the pennies that were scattered all over the tunnel. "Well, I suspect that we have a long, arduous task ahead of us," he said. "We'll have to inspect every one of these pennies, penny by penny, until we find the Coolidge-head penny. Naturally, it will be the last one we look at."

"Then," the prospector began, "why don't we start with—"

"Forget it," Max told him. "I used that line when we were discussing tunnels." He looked up toward the ceiling—or floor—again. "Finding that penny and signalling to the Chief is the only way we'll ever get out of here," he said. "The old prospector is right—even standing on a mule I couldn't reach that floor."

Max, 99 and the old prospector began inspecting the pennies.

"It's not this one," Max said, tossing the first penny aside.

"Nor this," 99 said, doing the same to the first penny she had picked up.

"I got it!" the old prospector shouted.

Max took the penny from him. "That's Lincoln upside-down," he said.

"Oh. Sorry. Sure looked like Coolidge right-side-up to me."

The search for the special penny continued. Max, 99 and the old man inspected coin after coin after coin after coin after coin, tossing each one aside after looking at it. Several hours later, Max halted because his vision was blurring. While he rested his eyes, he watched 99 and the old prospector as they continued the sorting.

"Hold it," Max said wearily after a few minutes.

"What's the matter, Max?"

"99, the old prospector is looking at coins and tossing them into one pile, and you are taking from that pile and tossing them into another pile. I have been taking from the pile that you've been tossing them into, and I've been tossing them into another pile—the pile that the old prospector has been taking from. Do you realize what we've been doing?"

"We've all been looking at the same coins. Max, over and over again."

"I'm afraid so, 99," Max nodded. "We'll have to start again."

The three moved farther apart, then resumed the search. For hours and hours they inspected coin after coin, and found nothing that even closely resembled a

Coolidge-head penny. Eventually, Max stopped again. He looked at his watch.

"It's dawn," he announced.

99 sighed defeatedly. "And we still have thousands of pennies to look at," he said. "Max, if Arbuthnot and those other assassins are leaving today, our mission will be a failure. We'll still be sorting pennies for days yet."

"You're right, 99. I think we'll have to find some other way to escape. Old man," he said to the old prospector, "what's the chance of finding another exit from this mine? I've seen a lot of movies with long lost mines in them, and in some of them a secret exit has been found. Nobody knew anything about it until the hero and heroine blundered upon it by chance. Have you by any chance blundered upon anything like that?"

The old prospector shook his head. "If there was a secret exit, I wouldn't have found it," he said. "Abe Shuster and Mabel Wamsutter would've blundered upon it by chance. And, the fact is, they didn't."

"All right, that eliminates that possibility," Max said. "Let's try to think of something else." He guestured. "In the meantime, you two continue inspecting the coins," he said. "If I can't think of an alternative, we'll have to depend on trying to get a squad of Control agents to town to look for us."

"Trying?" the old prospector said. "The way you talked about it before, it sounded like a dead cinch."

"From now on, shall we not use that word?" Max asked.

"Sorry," the old prospector replied. "I've been away from civilization a long time, you know. I had no idea a word like 'cinch' had become offensive. I won't say it again."

While 99 and the old prospector continued the hunt for the Coolidge-head penny, Max paced back and

forth in the tunnel, trying to think of another and
quicker way out. Once, he stopped and then charged
the tunnel wall. But it did not give, and all he got out
of the effort was a bruised shoulder. Another time, he
stood under the shaft of light and stared upward and
was heard to mutter something addressed to someone
called the sacred god of Good Guydom. That attempt
was even less successful than the other, however, since
he didn't even get a bruised shoulder out of it.

"That's it!" Max suddenly cried.

"What, Max?" 99 asked, rising.

"Something the old prospector said several hours
ago," Max replied. "He gave me the solution—I just
didn't realize it at the time!"

"But what, Max?"

"He said I couldn't reach the crack in the floor even
standing on a mule's back!"

"Yup, that's what I said," the old prospector agreed.
"If it's that much help to you, I'll say it again. Why,
you couldn't reach that crack—"

"Once was enough," Max broke in. "Actually, that
isn't the solution. But it gave me the idea for the solution. It's true that I couldn't reach the crack by standing on a mule's back. But, why couldn't I reach the
crack by standing on a mule's back standing on a pile
of pennies?"

"Max . . . could you explain that?"

"First, 99, we'll position the mule under the crack,"
Max explained. "Then we'll pile the pennies on the
mule's back. And then I'll stand on the pile of pennies."

"It won't work, Max," 99 told him. "Those pennies
won't stay on the mule's—" She looked suddenly
thoughtful. "But, what we could do," she said, "is get
the mule to stand on the pennies. That would raise the
mule up. Then, standing on the mule's back, you
would be higher, too."

"Well, yes, I guess that would work—if you want to do it the hard way," Max said. "All right, let's get all these pennies together again in a big pile."

99 looked a little doubtful. "After all this sorting we've done, Max? What if we find out after we pile the pennies up and get the mule to stand on the pile that you still can't reach the crack?"

"That's simple, 99. I don't know why you can't figure it out yourself. We'll simply start sorting the pennies again."

"I know, Max, but—" She shrugged. "All right, we'll do it your way."

Max, 99 and the old prospector began heaping the pennies into one huge pile. The project did not take long. But the pile was no help. Because it had been piled up several yards from the spot under the crack in the floor. They then spent a considerable amount of time moving the pile to where, theoretically, it would do some good.

"Perfect!" Max announced when the pennies were piled beneath the crack. "Now, all we have to do is to get the mule to stand on it." He addressed Madame DuBarry. "I just hope you understand how important your part in this is," he said. "It's my intention, you see, to stand on your back and reach up and remove those floor boards. Then, I can climb up into the saloon. And, once up there, I can reach down and pull 99 up. Is that clear?"

"Hee-haw!"

"Yes, it *is* true that I won't be able to haul you up. But, then, you're a ghost. All you have to do to get out of here is disappear here and reappear somewhere else. Not being a ghost, however, I don't have that advantage. And that's why it's so important for you to stand on that pile of pennies. Now, you just climb up there, then I'll climb up onto your back. If it seems too complicated to you, don't think about it. Just do it."

"Hee-haw!"

"I apologize," Max said. "I'm sure you're a very intelligent mule."

The mule snorted, then climbed to the top of the mound of pennies.

"Max, it works!" 99 said, surprised.

"I sort of resent that tone, 99," Max said. "The mule didn't doubt it for a minute."

Max climbed the pile of pennies, too. Then he got up on Madame DuBarry's back. Balancing precariously, he stretched, trying to reach the crack in the floor above.

"Max . . ." 99 said hopefully.

Max sighed glumly. "I'm afraid not, 99," he reported. "Just a few more inches and . . . no, I just can't reach it." He sat back down on the mule. "I guess it's back to sorting pennies, 99," he said apologetically.

"Don't get down yet," the old prospector said. "Might be I can help. You sure you want to get out of here? It's not too bad a life in this mine, you know. There's hardly any traffic to speak of. And you never have to worry about accidentally falling into a mine— seeing as how you're already in one."

"Don't get the wrong idea—it sounds lovely," Max said. "But we have a duty to perform. And the only way we can do it is by getting out of here. If you can help, please do."

"Okay. You asked for it."

The old prospector walked around behind Madame DuBarry and gave him a swift kick in the tail. The mule bucked, raring up, and tossed Max straight up through the floor. There was a splintering sound as the planks shattered. Then there was a loud thump. Then silence.

"That elevator'll give you a rough ride sometimes," the old prospector commented.

"Max!" 99 cried, calling up through the hole in the floor. "Max! Where are you? Are you all right?"

Max's face appeared at the rim of the hole. "I have a bruised shoulder all over, 99," he said. "But I still appear to be in one piece." He reached a hand down through the opening. "Get up on the mule," he said, "and I'll pull you out."

"Do you see the KAOS assassins anywhere around, Max?" 99 asked, climbing up onto Madame DuBarry's back.

"I haven't looked yet," Max replied. "But I don't hear anything. In fact, it sounds ominously quiet up here."

"That's the mice," the old prospector said.

"I haven't seen any mice," Max replied.

"We haven't got any. That's what makes them so quiet."

"Oh."

99 stretched, reaching up, and Max got hold of her hand, then hauled her up out of the mine. When they were both in the saloon, then looked back down into the tunnel at the old prospector and Madame DuBarry.

"Are you going to join us?" Max asked. "This will be the exciting part coming up. It's where we good guys foil the bad guys. There's usually a lot of action."

" 'Bout time," the old prospector said. "But . . . I guess I'll just skip it. I'm not as young as I used to be. Too much excitement isn't good for me."

"What, exactly, could happen to you?" Max asked. "After all, you're already—"

"Max . . . don't ask personal questions," 99 whispered. "Maybe he's sensitive about being you-know-what."

"I don't know why he should be," Max said. "Nobody would even guess. He doesn't look you-know-what." He addressed the old prospector again. "This is probably good-bye, then," he said. "We're going to try to capture the KAOS assassins double-handed. Without the Coolidge-head penny, we have no way of communicating with the Chief. And, after we take them into custody, we'll want to get them back to Washington as quickly as possible. That won't leave any time for a formal farewell. So—"

"Max! They're gone!"

"Yes. Disappeared," Max nodded, rising. "Well, I don't blame them. I guess you didn't notice, 99, but I was sort of working up to a farewell speech. I figured if I wouldn't have time later, then— But, fortunately, the old prospector saw what was coming and took appropriate action. Now, let's you and I do the same thing."

Max and 99 hurried to the door of the saloon. Then, cautiously, they peered out. The dusty streets were deserted.

"We're in luck, 99," Max whispered. "They're probably all over at the hotel packing. Maybe we can take them by surprise."

"I hope so, Max."

They crept out of the saloon and carefully made their way toward the hotel, staying close to the buildings, moving slowly and warily, not wanting to make any unnecessary sound. A short time later, they reached the porch of the hotel. There, they stood silently by the doorway for a while, listening. But no sound came from within.

"They're all upstairs!" Max whispered.

"Max . . . do you suppose—"

"Shhhhh!"

Max motioned, then entered the hotel lobby and crossed toward the stairs, with 99 following close behind. When they got to the steps, they halted once more. Max pressed a finger to his lips to warn 99 to be especially quiet. Then, carefully, step by step, they proceeded upward. Soon, they reached the second floor. After a brief pause to take in a deep breath and let it out, they moved on to the first room. With great care, Max opened the door and looked in. The room was empty. He closed the door and they proceeded to the second room. It was empty, too. So was the third room, and the fourth room, and the fifth room, and—

"Max, *all* of the rooms are empty!" 99 said, ceasing to whisper. "They've gone!"

"Let's not jump to conclusions, 99," Max said, looking uncomfortable. "Maybe they all just stepped out for a minute. They're probably all at the corner newsstand. Or perhaps—"

"Max, they're gone!"

"They could be having breakfast in the dining room, 99."

"But all the baggage is gone, Max. You mean they took their suitcases to breakfast."

"Maybe they're late. Maybe they have to catch a train. Maybe—"

From outside came the whistle of a train.

Then a voice called out. " 'Board! All Aboard!"

"Max—the train!"

"Hurry, 99!" Max shouted, racing toward the stairs. "That's our ride back to Washington!"

11.

Max and 99 dashed from the hotel and ran up the street to the railroad station. Just as they reached it, they saw the conductor get aboard the train, then enter a car. Max and 99 jumped aboard, too. Max, with 99 right behind him, threw open the door of the car. Facing him, smiling cordially, was the conductor, who was pointing a pistol at him.

"Sorry," Max said briskly, "but I've got to keep up the momentum. If I slow down, I'll miss the beat, and then I'll have to start at the beginning again—dum, dum, de, dum, dum, dum!"

On the final "dum," Max swung his arm and delivered a karate chop to the wrist of the conductor. The gun clattered to the floor. As the conductor reached for it, Max dum, dum, de, dum, dum, dummed once more, and, at the same time, drove a knee into the conductor's chest, flipping him over backwards. The conductor landed on his back—flat. From that position, he peered at Max blearily, while Max picked up the pistol.

"Sorry, again," Max said.

"Don't apologize," the conductor replied. "It was worth it to hear a great sound like that." Then he collapsed, unconscious.

"Where to now, Max?" 99 asked.

"To find Arbuthnot," Max answered, moving forward along the aisle, now in possession of the gun.

"But, Max, it's a long train," 99 said, following him again. "And we don't know where he is."

"Logic will take us to him, 99," Max said. "We know he's just concluded a grueling few days. This seminar has probably sapped every ounce of physical and mental energy he had. So, now, he'll be resting. Or, as the railroad men say, lounging. Consequently, I'm fairly positive that we'll find him in the lounge car."

"Max, I think you're probably right. But . . . why are we going this way?"

Max halted. "To the lounge car, 99. I just explained that. Remember the part about every sap being grueled after all— No, I mean about—"

"Max, I know," 99 broke in. "What I meant was, the lounge car is located in the other direction. You're heading toward the engine."

"Logic only tells where, it doesn't tell how to get there, 99," Max said. Then he turned and led the way in the other direction. "Now, when we get there and find Arbuthnot relaxing alone in the lounge car," Max said, "I'll rush in and overpower him and—"

"Max, you have a pistol now," 99 pointed out.

"Oh." He looked at the gun in his hand. "Yes, that's right, I do. All right, then, I'll saunter in and get the drop on him. Then I'll order him to summon all the other KAOS assassins, and we'll keep them prisoner in the lounge car until we get back to Washington. How does that sound to you, 99?"

"Who'll drive the train, Max?"

"The train driver."

"But he's a KAOS agent, Max. Won't he—"

"All right, I'll drive the train, 99. It couldn't be too difficult. I mean, there are those tracks to follow. And the route is probably very well marked."

"But who will keep the KAOS assassins prisoner?"

"You will, 99. I'll give you the gun and you— Oh-oh, here we are, 99. This next car is the lounge car. Stay here—I'll go peek in and make sure Arbuthnot is in there." Leaving 99, Max crept forward. When he reached the door of the lounge car he opened it a crack and looked in. Then he closed it and returned to where 99 was waiting. "This is going better than I expected," he said. "We won't have to get Arbuthnot to summon all the KAOS assassins to the lounge car. They're all in there now."

"Max! All of them? That's an awful lot of KAOS assassins for just two of us to handle."

"99, don't worry. We've got the momentum going. Just keep up the rhythm and we can't fail. Now . . . ready? Dum, dum, de, dum, dum, dum!"

Max and 99 advanced to the door of the lounge car. Max repeated the beat—dum, dum, de, dum, dum, dum—then he flung open the door and he and 99 rushed in, catching Arbuthnot completely by surprise.

"Dum, dum, dum, de— Ooops! Uh, dum, de, dum— No, it goes, dum, dum, dum, dum, dum, dum, dum—"

Max had lost the momentum.

"Get 'em!" Arbuthnot commanded.

A KAOS assassin threw a block at Max, hit him across the mid-section, and drove him all the way out the door and several cars back. Recovering, Max threw a block at the KAOS assassin, hitting him more-or-less in the mid-section (around the ankles) and driving him all the way back to the lounge car. When they arrived, Max saw that 99 had been overpowered. So, alone, he tackled the entire group of KAOS assassins.

It was a short battle, however. Max raised an arm to karate chop Arbuthnot, hoping to gain a psychological advantage by putting the leader out of action. But at that same moment, hoping to gain an actual advantage, one of the KAOS assassins popped him on the back of the skull with the butt of a pistol, dropping him in the aisle. Surrendering to the logic of the situation, Max became immediately unconscious.

A few moments later, when Max recovered, he saw Arbuthnot standing over him, holding a gun on him. Max thought fast. "Watch out! That's the gun *I* had!" he shouted at Arbuthnot. "All my germs are crawling on it!"

Arbuthnot stared at the pistol in horror for a second. Then he screeched and threw it into the air and ran to the KAOS assassin who was in charge of the spray bottle. "Spray me! Spray me!" he ordered frantically.

Max, meanwhile, leaped to his feet. He snatched the gun from the air. And by the time Arbuthnot had been disinfected, Max had taken charge, covering the KAOS assassins with the pistol.

"Max, that was marvelous!" 99 cried delightedly, breaking away from the KAOS agent who had been holding her.

"That's very frank of you, 99," Max replied. "Now, I'm sure these assassins have some tape or some rope around here somewhere. If you'll just—"

There was a hissing sound from the front end of the train. Then the whole string of cars was suddenly jolted. Max and 99 and the KAOS assassins were all thrown off balance. The gun that Max had managed to regain went flying. Max and 99 and all the KAOS assassins scrambled after it.

"No! Don't! Don't touch it!" Arbuthnot screeched. "It's full of germs!"

They all drew back, leaving the pistol in the middle of the aisle.

"Max, what are we doing?" 99 said. *"We're* not afraid of germs!"

By then, however, it was too late. The KAOS assassins had all drawn their own guns. And all of the guns were pointed at Max and 99.

"I suppose you're wondering where that jerk came from," Arbuthnot said to Max and 99. "That was my engineer."

"He certainly is," Max replied grumpily.

"He was practicing," Arbuthnot went on. "Fortunately—for us—he always starts off with a jerk."

"He certainly is," Max said again.

Arbuthnot addressed one of the other KAOS assassins. "I'll have a disinfected gun," he said.

The assassin handed him a pistol.

"And now," Arbuthnot said, speaking to all the assassins, "I will show you the one assassination method that I did not mention during the seminar. Normally, I wouldn't be caught dead using it. It's too crude . . . too . . . too . . . uhhhhh! But, it does have two advantages—it's simple and it's quick."

"He's talking about just walking up to the victim and shooting him between the eyes," Max explained to the KAOS assassins. "He's right—it's crude. But, if done well, it can be fascinating to watch." He turned to Arbuthnot. "You do it well, I suppose."

"Superbly."

"Then, watch this very carefully," Max said to the other assassins. "It will be worth seeing."

"Max! You sound as if you're looking forward to it!" 99 said.

"I always enjoy watching an expert at work."

Arbuthnot raised the pistol and pointed it at Max, sighting straight between the eyes. "On the count of three," he said. "One . . . two . . .—"

There was a distant rumbling sound.

Arbuthnot frowned, and, lowering the pistol, said, "What was that?"

"Thunder, I think," Max said. "Gee, I hope it doesn't rain."

"No . . . it wasn't thunder," Arbuthnot said. He went to the door of the lounge car and opened it and looked out—then screamed. "Oh, no!"

The rumbling became a thundering. Then the burly girls who had been on the train earlier came stomping into the car. They set upon the KAOS agents, attacking them with fury and abandon.

Max grabbed 99 by the hand and they dived behind a lounge chair. From there, they watched as the lady wrestlers mauled the assassins. KAOS agents were everywhere, flying through the air, skidding up the aisle on their noses, necks, ears and other parts. KAOS agents crashed through windows and were hurled through doorways. KAOS agents were kicked, bitten, pinched, punched, and pulled and pummeled.

"Fortunately for us, they're wrestlers first and ladies last," Max said to 99.

"Max, where did they come from? Why are they so outraged?"

"I think we'll soon find out, 99. They seem to be running out of KAOS assassins to kick, bite, pinch, punch, pull and pummel."

The lounge car suddenly became quiet. KAOS assassins were sprawled everywhere, unconscious.

Max and 99 raised up from behind the lounge chair.

Several burly girls started after them.

"Stop!" the leader of the wrestlers commanded. "We're in enough trouble as it is, ladies," she said, looking suddenly worried.

"Trouble?" Max said.

"This is always happening," the lady wrestler replied. "We get a little peeved at somebody, and we break all their arms and legs. And, it seems, in a riled up world like the world we live in today, nobody's got any sense of humor any more. They get mad at us for breaking their arms and legs and sue us for damages and threaten to put us in jail and all like that there."

"I think I have some rather pleasant news for you," Max said. "You may not get many laughs out of this mayhem you committed today, but, on the other hand, you may get a medal."

Max then explained that he and 99 were Control agents and that the men the ladies had mauled were KAOS assassins. The lady wrestlers were delighted by the news. They wanted to kick the assassins a few more times for good measure while they were unconscious. But Max felt that would be adding injury to injury, and he restrained them.

"What baffles me," Max said, "is why you weren't all killed when you were dropped off the train through that false door in the dining car."

"Why, it was just a normal fall for us," the leader of the lady wrestlers replied. "In our profession, we're used to falls."

"Yes . . . I can see that," Max nodded. "How did you find us, though, here in this ghost town?"

"No problem," the lady wrestler replied. "It's not hard to follow a train, you know. It leaves tracks."

"I don't know why I didn't think of that," Max nodded. "Well," he said, "that seems to wrap up the case fairly neatly. I'll just trot up to the engine and overpower the engineer, then I'll drive the train back to Washington, and we'll deliver all these KAOS assassins to the proper authorities."

"Let us!" the leader of the lady wrestlers begged.

"Let you what?"

"Overpower the engineer," she replied. "If we're not going to get sued for this, we can really let go. We kind of need the relaxation. We've been jogging for days to catch up with this train."

"Well . . ."

"And we'll drive the train back to Washington, too," the leader of the burly girls said. "You probably want a rest yourself."

"As a matter of fact—"

"Come on, Max, before they change their minds," 99 said. She took him by the hand and drew him out of the lounge car and along the aisle toward their compartment. "We've worked hard," she said. "We deserve a few hours off."

"I suppose you're right, 99."

They reached the compartment and entered. Then sat down in the seats, facing each other. A few moments later, the sound of screaming came from the front of the train.

"I think we're changing engineers," Max commented.

99 nodded. "I feel so secure with those lady wrestlers in charge," she said.

"Yes," Max began, "I think from here on out, 99, it will be smooth—"

There was a sound like a puff of air. Then Max suddenly found a mule in his lap.

"99!" he shouted, shoving Madame DuBarry. "This animal got away from its keeper."

"No, he didn't!" the voice of the old prospector replied. "Here I am, right over here."

"He's on my lap, Max!" 99 reported.

"If you're going to ride in this compartment, you'll have to sit in the seats!" Max insisted. "What are you doing here, anyway?"

The old prospector and Madame DuBarry moved from Max's and 99's laps. The prospector sat alongside 99. The mule lay down on the floor between the seats. At the same moment, the train started moving.

"All ashore who's going ashore!" Max said. "It was very nice of you to come to the train to see us off, but you better leave now. This train is on its way to Washington."

"Yup!" the old prospector said. "Us, too. Me and Madame DuBarry."

"Oh, no!" Max said glumly.

"Yup!" the old prospector said again. "After all these centuries—"

"Decades," 99 corrected.

"No, it hasn't been that long," the old prospector said. "It's seemed like it, though, sometimes. Anyway, as I was saying, after all these centuries of living the lonely life, searching for that long lost gold, we decided to kick up our heels and do a little livin'. So, we're moving to the city."

"There'll be a lot of problems of adjustment," Max said, trying to discourage them.

"We figure we'll just stick by you and do what you do," the old prospector said. " 'Till we get the hang of it, that is."

"And where will you stay?" Max said. "There aren't many landladies in Washington who will rent to a ghost and a mule. Now, if you had an elephant with you— But a mule, these days, uh-huh."

"That won't be no problem," the old prospector replied. "We figure we'll just bunk with you. You got a place, haven't you?"

"Well, yes, but—"

"Tit for tat," the old prospector said. "We shared our long lost mine with you, so we figure you'll be just as happy as all get-out to share your home with us. 'Cause you're folks."

"Well, yes, I guess we are, but—"

"Oh, Max!" 99 said. "It's not the best way to start married life, sharing an apartment with an old prospector and a mule, both ghosts."

"Look on the bright side, 99. It could be worse."
"How, Max?"
"It could be a relative."
99 tried hard not to look the way she felt.

If you enjoyed this book, you will want to read these other absorbing TEMPO BOOKS

THE PUSHCART WAR, by Jean Merrill. The historical (hysterical) story of New York's Pushcart War of 1976 . . . including the Daffodil Massacre and the Pea Shooter Campaign.   4804   60¢

SINBAD AND ME, by Kin Platt. A really smart English bulldog helps his master unravel mysteries in this hilarious puzzler.   4861   50¢

BEETLE BAILEY, by Mort Walker. The misadventures of the wackiest "G.I." in the Army—from America's Number 1 comic strip.   4884   75¢

FALL OUT LAUGHING, BEETLE BAILEY, by Mort Walker. More madcap misadventures of Beetle and his zany friends and foes.   5305   75¢

TIGER, by Bud Blake. A wildly funny collection from America's newest comic strip sensation, *Tiger.*   5312   60¢

RED SKELTON'S FAVORITE GHOST STORIES. A scary spookfest of shivery tales selected and edited by America's madcap master of mirth.   4882   75¢

ROD SERLING'S TWILIGHT ZONE REVISITED. A new collection of startling explorations into the realm of the supernatural.   4871   60¢

ROD SERLING'S THE TWILIGHT ZONE. Weird tales of bizarre events too strange to be believed, yet too grippingly real to be doubted.   4789   60¢

CUSTER'S LAST STAND, by Will Henry. The incredible true story of the events that led up to the greatest cavalry and Indian battle of frontier history—the Battle of the Little Big Horn.   4881   75¢

BURIED TREASURE IN THE U. S. And Where to Find It, by Thomas Penfield. Exciting true tales of pirates, prospectors and fabulous fortunes —plus a list of 807 lost treasures.   5303   75¢

THREE MEN ON THIRD, by Gene Olson. When a wacky team has a coach who doesn't know a home run from a hypotenuse, the ball game is strictly for laughs.   4826   50¢

ANDY BUCKRAM'S TIN MEN, by Carol R. Brink. Andy builds four robots—then finds himself marooned with them on a deserted island!   4851   50¢

THE GNOMOBILE, by Upton Sinclair. The merry, madcap adventures of Elizabeth and Rodney and two delightful gnomes in search of a home.   4812   50¢

FRIDAY'S TUNNEL, by John Verney. The zany Callendar family—an offbeat crew of eight—gets caught up in an international crisis of intrigue and espionage.   4870   60¢

FEBRUARY'S ROAD, by John Verney. Another sparkling adventure—loaded with mirth and mystery—starring the amazing Callendar family.   5311   60¢

THE STORY CATCHER, by Mari Sandoz. The moving story of the way an Indian boy proved himself a man in the eyes of his people.   4790   50¢

TO BUILD A LAND, by Sally Watson. This is the stirring story of the young people who worked and struggled to make Israel live and become a nation.   4873   60¢

ACROSS FIVE APRILS, by Irene Hunt. Young Jethro was forced to set his boyhood aside during the five fateful years of the Civil War.   4798   60¢

PENROD, by Booth Tarkington. The sidesplitting story about the Worst Boy in Town.   5322   75¢

THE WIND IN THE WILLOWS, by Kenneth Graham. The best loved, classic story of the adventures of boastful, extravagant Mr. Toad and his long-suffering wildwood friends.   4841   50¢

THE JUNGLE BOOK, by Rudyard Kipling. Saved from the jaws of Shere Khan, Mowgli is raised by Mother Wolf as one of her own cubs.   4867   50¢

FLOATING ISLAND, by Anne Parrish. Cast away   4890 60¢
on a tropical island, a family of dolls finds
beauty, fun and great adventure.

THE GLASS SLIPPER, by Eleanor Farjeon. A de-   4863 50¢
lightful retelling of the romance of the glass
slipper—the enchanted story of a love that
turned a kitchen maid into a princess.

and these HENRY REED books
by Keith Robertson

HENRY REED, INC. This serious journal of Henry's   4856 60¢
wildly funny business enterprises makes a
hilarious book.

HENRY REED'S JOURNEY. Henry's search for fire-   4857 50¢
works takes him and Midge on the funniest
coast-to-coast tour ever.

HENRY REED'S BABY-SITTING SERVICE. Henry   4858 50¢
could handle the babies, but a peacock really
makes the feathers fly!

If your dealer does not have the books you want, **ORDER** from
TEMPO BOOKS, 51 Madison Avenue, New York, N.Y. 10010
enclosing check or money order—no currency or C.O.D.'s
please. Please include 10¢ per book for postage and handling.
A complete list of titles is available upon request.